MW01132726

HER DREAM DATE BOSS

Billionaire Boss Romance: Steele Family Romance

CAMI CHECKETTS

Birch River
PUBLISHING

COPYRIGHT

Her Dream Date Boss: Billionaire Boss Romances: Steele Family Romance

Copyright © 2019 by Cami Checketts

All rights reserved.

No part of this book may be reproduced in any form or by any electronic or mechanical means, including information storage and retrieval systems, without written permission from the author, except for the use of brief quotations in a book review.

DEDICATION

To my sister, Abbie. Mae in her funny t-shirts reminded me so much of you. Thanks for making me laugh and always being there for me.

FREE BOOK

Sign up for Cami's VIP newsletter and receive a free ebook copy of *The Resilient One: A Billionaire Bride Pact Romance* here.

You can also receive a free copy of *Rescued by Love: Park City Firefighter Romance* by clicking here and signing up for Cami's newsletter.

CHAPTER ONE

Mae Delaney refastened her long, dark hair into its standard ponytail, pushed her large glasses firmly into place, smoothed down one of her favorite T-shirts, and made sure the screen angle didn't show she was in yoga pants at two p.m. She ran some pineapple lip gloss over her lips and practiced her smile in the mirror. "Look at you, you stinking hottie. You're going to slaughter him." The self-talk helped a tiny bit. She was the furthest thing from hot, and her thick glasses made it impossible to see her dark eyes, which her best friend, Kit, reassured her were her best feature.

Her stomach fluttering, she pushed the button on video chat to call Slade Steele: the most charming and handsome man on the planet, owner of Steele Wholesale Lending, and her boss.

Slade's perfectly sculpted face filled the screen, complemented by his deep brown eyes with lashes longer than her own and a trimmed beard that only served to highlight his intriguing lips.

He was gorgeous but so down-to-earth and kind. She scoured
the internet nightly for Slade Steele sightings. Over the last few
months, she'd seen him on humanitarian trips with his church,
helping a child who'd lost his mom at a hockey game, taking his
beautiful little sister who had Down syndrome to the premiere
of a chick flick, and playing rugby with teenage boys at the park.
In one of the rugby pictures, he'd had his shirt off. She sighed
inadvertently.

"Hi, Mae. How are you today?"

"If I was any better, I'd be exalted already," she said.

He chuckled. "Well, lucky for me, you're still on this planet."

"Lucky, lucky you. Do you ever stop and thank the good Lord
that you get the blessing of talking to me most days of
the week?"

He grinned. "Yes, ma'am, I do." His eyes trailed over her T-shirt,
and he read it out loud. "People in sleeping bags ... are the soft
tacos of the bear world." Chuckling, he said, "Does that mean
you have an aversion to tacos?"

"No, sir. I like tacos. I just don't want to be a taco."

He grinned. "Good to know."

All of Mae's nerves settled, replaced with a deep longing to track
him down, throw herself against his well-formed chest, kiss him
good and long, and tell him she'd loved him for almost two years
now. Then maybe they could go for tacos. But thinking about his
well-formed chest ... Could she touch it at their first meeting, or
would that be an inappropriate action for a good Christian girl?
She'd never really dated, so she had no idea. Hmm. It might be

worth it. She might not get exalted as quickly, but she could repent later.

"Mae. Mae?"

"What? What just happened? Is it hot in here?" She fanned her face.

Slade laughed. "I'm not sure what your weather is like in Sausalito, so I have no idea. It's steamy hot in Boston."

Steamy hot? Oh, my. She wanted him to say those words again. Even better, maybe he could say them after they kissed the first time. *Focus, Mae.* "Dang man reminding me of the sad state of my life."

"What's that?"

"Never being where you are."

Slade's cheek twitched as if he was holding back laughter. "Can we get back to that state in a moment? I need some help from my best account rep."

"Of course you do. It's the only reason you ever call me." Of course he'd never call her for any reason but work. He was the perfect male model who dated the perfect female models. He lived in a different world than she did. At least she had these short conversations most days of the week, and she could dream of him.

"Must I remind you that you called me?" He winked, and Mae had to fan herself again.

"Stop flirting with me and tell me what the problem is."

Slade smiled, probably thinking he'd never flirt with the likes of her, but he was too classy to say that. He began listing for her which branches were having issues she needed to resolve. She was the liaison between his lending companies and the local mortgage companies. Mae typed away into her computer as he spoke.

"You know you could email me most of this?" Mae said, though she immediately regretted it.

"Don't say that. Then I would miss out on my daily dose of Mae humor."

"I'm actually funnier with my fingertips."

He blinked at her. "Hmm. Maybe I'll try email tomorrow."

"Please don't. I like seeing your handsome face." Her neck was burning, and she prayed that he wouldn't call her out or fire her for inappropriate talking in the workplace. But she worked remotely and he was the owner, so hopefully her blatant flirtations were okay.

"You're the one that suggested email."

"Forgive me. My brain vacates its lovely home when I stare into those deep brown eyes."

"Ah, Mae." He gifted her with his earth-moving smile. "You're good for the self-esteem. Hey, I've gotta run. I'm actually flying into San Francisco in a few hours. Do you want to get together for lunch or dinner tomorrow? I'll come across the bay to Sausalito."

Mae froze. Her stomach was swirling like it was full of butterflies, and her mouth and throat were so dry she couldn't even swallow. Slade Steele was coming to San Francisco, and he wanted to go to lunch or dinner with her?

Oh my goodness! Oh my goodness!

What should she do? Her brain whirled—play it cool, get a drink of water, find a firefighter to drench her with his hose, or call her sassy best friend Kit and have her come answer him? That would take too long, though, and he was staring at her, awaiting her answer. Mae tried to squeak out a yes, but nothing came out.

"Maybe not the best idea?" Slade asked, his dark eyes filling with concern.

If Mae missed this opportunity, Kit would sentence her to a year of walking lunges or some other exercise torture. Kit forced her to attend her boot camp class each morning, and it never got easier for Mae.

Slade waited, one perfect eyebrow arched up. "It's all right, Mae—"

"I'll go to dinner with you!" she yelled. "Yes!" Hallelujah. Praise every saintly ancestor she didn't even know and her beloved family watching from up above. She'd finally found her tongue and answered affirmatively, if a bit too eagerly.

Slade smiled. "All right. Text me where and when."

"B-but I don't know what you like to eat." Or how fancy he wanted to go or how intimate she could get away with. She'd said she liked tacos, but had he ever said he liked them also? Should she really force him to come over to Sausalito, or should she get brave and go into the city? She wasn't a recluse; she simply enjoyed the more quiet side of the bay. Okay, truthfully, she was petrified to drive across the Golden Gate Bridge.

"It's your city," he said, "so you're the expert, and I like everything. Talk to you tomorrow."

He ended the call like he did everything—decisive, in control, and so stinking sexy. When his handsome face disappeared, Mae leaned back and all of the oxygen fled her body. She was going to dinner with Slade! She wanted to dance around, call Kit, drink a Diet Coke, and then go for a walk through her beautiful town.

Instead, Mae sat there, staring at her computer's background of a gorgeous waterfall with thick greenery surrounding it. The only waterfall she'd ever been to was in Mill Valley, up the road from her hometown of Sausalito. She hadn't traveled outside of northern California since she was fourteen, but that was all right. Her home was a beautiful spot.

She glanced around her family home. As the only surviving member of her family, she'd inherited the house when she turned eighteen. Luckily Kit's parents had been her guardians when her family was killed. Living with them the last three years of high school had been good. She'd overheard Kit's mom once telling a friend on the phone how tragic it was that Mae refused to drive a car or go to the city, but Mae knew that she'd said it out of concern. Kit's family had been nothing but kind to her, and she loved them. Mae knew she was strange and probably hard to deal with. She feared the bridge and most kinds of traveling. She didn't know how to conquer those fears, and thankfully Kit and her family hadn't ever forced her. Even Kit's older brothers, who loved to tease her and Kit about everything, had left her alone about it.

As Mae focused on a picture of her and her younger sisters standing with their bikes on the trail that continued to Mill Valley, she felt a pang of loneliness. She loved living in this house. She loved the view of the bay out her large windows and the open layout of the house. She loved the memories. She didn't love being alone.

Sighing, she forced herself to focus on the work Slade had just given her. It'd take a few hours, but she'd be done in time to meet Kit for an early dinner at Napa Valley Burger Company. Her stomach rumbled as she concentrated on her computer, but food could wait. She wouldn't let Slade down, and tomorrow she was going to finally meet him in person, go to dinner with the man of her dreams. Oh my goodness, she was so happy right now—and so terrified.

CHAPTER TWO

Slade Steele thanked his pilot and stewardess as he exited his airplane. A car was waiting to take him to his San Francisco offices. He regularly visited his fourteen branches spread throughout the U.S., but his home base was Boston. He hadn't been to San Francisco in over a year. It was a beautiful and diverse city, and he liked that it was right on the water like his hometown.

As Slade stared out the window, appreciating the view of the Golden Gate Bridge and the bay, he made a rash decision. "Can you take me across to Sausalito?" It was after five, and most of his employees would be gone for the day. He'd go walk the quaint streets of Sausalito and eat dinner there. He could meet with everyone he needed to tomorrow and then cap off his quick trip with dinner with Mae.

He smiled. Mae was hilarious and definitely not the type of woman he'd ever dated. He had never gotten a clear glimpse of her face or eyes because of the huge, thick glasses she wore. She was always in an oversized T-shirt with a funny saying on it, and she wore her hair pulled back in a ponytail.

Because of his own success and his family name, he was sought after by wealthy, powerful, and polished women. He'd dated his fair share, but he had yet to find someone who didn't take herself too seriously yet had enough substance to settle down with. He wanted a woman like his mama: fun, elegant, and independent, yet still able to lean on her husband and complement him.

They crossed the Golden Gate Bridge and drove through the thick trees on both sides of the road and down into Sausalito. He liked this area better than San Francisco; in his mind, it was quieter and had more character. He shouldn't second-guess why he was coming here. It wasn't as if he was going to find Mae. He could access employee records and show up at her door, but that might come across wrong. He wasn't looking for a romantic relationship with anyone right now; he was too focused on growing his business and being there for his little sister, Lottie, when he could. Lottie had started her own charity, Lottie's Loves, and it was his favorite pastime to work with her on it. But he really enjoyed teasing with Mae on their video chats, and there was something beautiful and graceful in the refined lines of her jawline and neck. Her lips were full and shiny whenever he talked to her. If only he could see her eyes, get the full picture of her face.

The driver pulled onto the quaint main street of Sausalito, the bay on the right-hand side. "Where to, sir?"

"Where's the best place for dinner?"

"Well, you have your fancy spots like Spinnaker, or there's a sushi place I've heard great things about, but you really can't go wrong with Napa Valley Burgers. Just depends what you're in the mood for, sir."

"A hamburger sounds perfect. Thanks."

"Of course."

They pulled up to a crowded restaurant with an open-air front and tables inside and out. The driver rushed around to get his door, and Slade palmed him a twenty. He was already paid a high hourly rate, but Slade liked to tip extra.

"Thank you, sir. Please text me if you need a ride back to your hotel later."

"I will. Thank you."

Slade strode into the restaurant, scanning the crowd for a dark ponytail, a frumpy T-shirt, and big glasses, but he didn't see her and knew he was being presumptuous. Mae had told him before that she was a hermit and rarely left her house. He was grateful she'd agreed to meet him for dinner tomorrow night. He had some silly visions of taking her glasses off, pulling her hair out of the ponytail, and finding in her deep brown eyes—well, he thought they'd be deep brown—the woman he'd always dreamed of.

Smiling, he realized he'd watched one too many chick flicks to humor sweet Lottie. It was ludicrous to fancy yourself in deep like with a person who you only knew through video chats.

"You want a table?" a teenage boy asked.

"Yes, thank you."

"This way."

He followed the young man through the restaurant, discarding his visions of tomorrow night. It would be a fun dinner with a friend and nothing more. He was too successful and driven to have time for anything else.

Mae adjusted her glasses, then tugged at her T-shirt. She'd showered and put on a clean T-shirt and a black cotton skirt. By her standards, she was dressed to kill. Still, she knew Kit would give her a hard time about her wardrobe. It wasn't that she didn't want to be attractive. Okay, maybe it was. She'd gotten a lot of attention from boys in middle school, but then her family had been killed and she'd hidden behind her thick glasses and frumpiness. It was easier and less risky to only let Kit in.

"'Bring me a Diet Coke and tell me I'm pretty'?" Kit strode up to her and rolled her eyes, pulling her in for a hug. "Has anyone ever done it?"

Mae grinned and puffed out her chest with the saying on her T-shirt. "Nope, but the man who does will be my soul mate."

Kit laughed and started steering her through the crowded restaurant back to her table. "Good luck finding him, then." Kit reached a corner table and sat, gesturing to the other chair.

Mae perched on the edge of the hard chair, took a long drink of the water waiting for her, and then exclaimed, "You won't believe me, but I'm going to dinner with my soul mate tomorrow night. Should I wear the shirt and see if he offers me a Diet Coke?"

Kit's eyebrows arched so high they almost touched her swooping blond locks. "You're ... going on a date?" The eyebrows settled, and her teal eyes filled with concern. "Truly?"

Mae forced a smile. "Truly."

"Someone asked you out?"

"Come on, it's getting hurtful now." She knew she was pathetic, but was she really *that* pathetic?

"Oh, sweetie." Kit leaned in and hugged her again. "I'm not trying to be rude. It's just you rarely leave the house, except to meet me for food or a workout. So, pray tell how some brilliant and lucky man found you and convinced you to leave the Bat Cave?"

Mae took some deep breaths, hardly able to contain her excitement at sharing who she was going out with. Kit knew all about her longtime crush, but her best friend understood the unreachable status of Slade Steele. He wasn't as well-known as his brother Preston, who played for the Georgia Patriots, or his brother Jex, who was an Instagram and YouTube star who got paid to do whatever insane stunt anyone challenged him to do. The youngest brother, Gunner, was in the military and got even less attention than Slade, who still got plenty of attention being a self-made billionaire and being too charming and handsome for anybody's good. No, Mae wasn't silly enough to believe Slade could ever return her feelings, but dinner with him would sustain her in the long, lonely years to come. Kit was right. Even if any man could compare to Slade for her, she'd never leave her house long enough to find him.

The waitress approached, interrupting Mae's chance to respond. She ordered a barbecue burger with a side of chips and guacamole; their guacamole was unreal, and she could already taste it. She hadn't eaten anything today, as she had a hard time eating after one of Kit's intense morning workouts, and then she'd become too distracted with work to think about food. The tantalizing smell of well-cooked meat was making her light-headed.

The waitress walked away, and Kit gasped and said in a breathless voice, "Slade Steele."

"How did you know?" Mae's gaze narrowed. Kit was in tune to Mae's deepest desires as her best and really only friend, but she wasn't telepathic.

Kit pointed, her eyes bugging out. "Slade Steele."

Mae followed her friend's finger, and her heart slammed against her chest. The man of her every desire was sitting across the crowded restaurant, eating by himself. Mae had never seen him in person, and he was glorious. Even eating a large hamburger, he managed to look suave and enticing.

She pressed a hand to her chest and tried to breathe in and out, in and out. "I'm going to hyperventilate," she muttered.

Kit grabbed her hand and squeezed it. "No, you're not. You're going to march over there and introduce yourself."

"I can't. I ... I'll pass out."

Kit growled at her. "You are doing this, now."

"B-but tomorrow." Oh, my, he was too perfect. In what alternate reality had she imagined she could go out with him? She glanced down at her ill-fitting, too-baggy clothes. She was truly a delusional idiot.

"I don't want to hear about tomorrow. You are doing this right now. You are talking to Slade Steele, and I'm going to watch like the proud best friend I am. If he's got even an ounce of sense in that handsome body, he'll be completely enthralled with you. Now, just to help him out a little bit ..."

Kit yanked Mae's glasses off. Mae blinked, but the instant fog didn't clear. "Can't see, truly can't see."

"Don't care, truly don't care. You are showing off those big brown eyes. And we're going to ... Hmm."

Mae imagined Kit tilted her head to the side, but it was all a blur. She was twice legally blind without her glasses and could only see things clearly a few inches away. Kit tugged at the elastic band holding her hair up. Mae's long hair spilled around her face. She liked her hair—it was soft and full—but it tickled her face and that bugged her.

Pushing at and fluffing Mae's hair, Kit made noises in her throat and clucked her tongue, but she didn't say much until she commanded, "Purse those lips, baby."

"No." Mae shrank away. She hated the feel of lipstick and always just stuck with gloss.

"You obey me, or you've lost your best friend," Kit commanded.

Mae knew it was an idle threat. They'd been best friends and neighbors since the womb. Destined since heaven to be friends, their moms used to say. She obediently pursed her lips instead of fighting. Best to get this over with. Get the meeting of her soul mate over with? Oh, good night! How was she going to march blindly across this restaurant and approach Slade? She wasn't ready, worthy, or confident enough. Her chest was feeling tighter and tighter.

A person walked up to their table and set plates down. "Here we are."

Mae caught a whiff of her favorite barbecue sauce and red meat cooked perfectly. She started salivating, despite the nerves racing through her body making her nauseated. "I need to eat something," she muttered around Kit putting gunk on her lips.

"No way. You're not going over there with barbecue breath or guacamole messing up this lipstick. Dang, that looks fabulous on you. Okay." Kit took both of Mae's hands and tugged her to her feet. She pulled her t-shirt tighter and tied it in a knot at her waist then rolled her skirt so it was a couple of inches shorter. "Yes. You're ready. Go slay that man, my beautiful friend."

"No, you don't understand. I'm feeling light-headed. I better eat something first." She reached blindly toward the food, but Kit swatted her hand.

"Get your tush over there. You can eat with him once you woo him. Be your funny, awesome self. You look gorgeous!" Kit squealed. "I'm so excited. This is truly a sign. You've always been the kindest person I know, and finally the good Lord is rewarding you!" Kit shoved her away from their table. "Go, girl, go!"

Mae unsteadily shuffled through the restaurant. She knew the general direction where Slade was sitting, but she'd have to get extremely close to see his face without her glasses. Getting close sounded fabulous; not being able to see his face clearly was a nightmare. Knowing Slade was light years out of her league and her romantic dreams could never end happily was a reality she had to live with.

She shuffled into the side of a chair, hitting her hip bone. "Ouch!"

"You okay?" a deep voice asked.

"Yes, thank you." It wasn't Slade's voice—there was no way she was even close to his location in the restaurant yet—so she started lumbering forward again.

A large palm wrapped around her elbow. "I'm Mike. I'd love to get your name," the same voice said.

Mae blinked up at the man—way, way up. He was tall like a giant and appeared handsome as far as she could distinguish. His voice was pleasant, and he smelled good, but she wasn't just looking for any guy to meet. She needed to get to Slade. "Mae," she murmured.

"I love your shirt, Mae," he continued. "If I bought you a Diet Coke, could I tell you how pretty you are?"

Mae smiled. Was this guy hitting on her? She hadn't been hit on in years. It felt nice, but she really, truly wanted to find Slade. No matter how nervous she was to meet him, she had to get to him. She was going to have dinner with him tomorrow night, but Kit was right: this was a sign from above, and she could hardly wait to be close to him, possibly build up some memories to treasure throughout her too-long life. What would he smell like? What would he feel like? Would they be as comfortable in their banter as they were through video chat? Her nerves were stretched thin and her stomach was tumbling, but this was her moment and she was ready to get in the game and start some serious flirting with the man of her dreams.

"I'm so sorry, but I'm meeting someone," she said.

"Oh. I understand. A woman as beautiful as you. Of course you're already taken."

She smiled at him. He truly thought she was beautiful. Maybe Kit had worked miracles. Maybe Slade actually would be interested in her and think she was beautiful like this blurry-faced, kind man did.

"Excuse me." Kit's voice. "She is taken, but I'd love that Diet Coke."

The man chuckled and released Mae's arm. "But you don't have the shirt."

"Take your shirt off and give it to me," Kit said to Mae.

"Oh my goodness, no." Mae rolled her eyes. "She doesn't need the shirt for you to tell her she's pretty," she said to the man. Kit was absolutely beautiful with her glossy, blond hair, teal-colored eyes, and smooth, tan skin, not to mention she was *the* fitness expert and a walking billboard for her gym.

"You're absolutely right. Can I buy you a Diet Coke?" Mike asked Kit, laughter in his voice.

"Absolutely," Kit said.

Mae nodded, her job here done. Kit could enjoy this kind man, another in the long line of men who floundered at Kit's feet, and Mae could get to Slade. She started his direction again, but hands grasped her shoulders.

"Wrong way, sweetie," Kit said, and she pushed her in the other direction.

The push was too hard, and Mae was unsteady; she flung out her hands and hit a tray. The server cursed as food, plates, and cups crashed to the ground.

"Oh, criminy!" Mae knelt and started helping pick stuff up and placing it onto the tray the server had dropped on the ground.

She heard Kit's and the man's voices as they helped also. They cleaned everything they could pick up, and the server said, "It's okay. I'll get a broom and mop to finish. Thanks." He bustled away.

Mae stood, feeling unsteady and stupid.

"Oh, no, you have barbecue sauce all over your shirt," Kit exclaimed, grabbing a napkin off the man's table and scrubbing at Mae's chest.

"Please give me my glasses back," Mae begged.

"No, Mae. You don't know how pretty you look without them."

Mae wanted to be attractive—who didn't?—but this was never

going to work. She couldn't blindly feel her way across the restaurant. Slade was a great guy and had never made her feel like the frumpy woman she was. Maybe he wouldn't think she was beautiful with her big glasses on, but he wouldn't be condescending to her either. "Please, Kit. This isn't working."

Long seconds passed. "Fine," Kit huffed, handing the glasses over.

Mae shoved them back on and was thrilled to have the world clear up again. She first saw Kit and the man who'd hit on her. Mike, that was it. He was extremely tall and extremely good-looking with short, tightly curled black hair, smooth brown skin, and amazing lips. Her confidence bolstered that he'd hit on her, but Kit was frowning.

"She shouldn't cover up her beautiful face, should she?" Kit asked Mike.

He shrugged his burly shoulders, obviously uncomfortable telling Mae she was ugly with the glasses, but he didn't appear to want to offend Kit either. "You have really amazing eyes, and the glasses cover them up."

"Thank you," Kit said. "My mom and I have been telling her that for years."

Mae inhaled sharply. "Okay, you two. I get it. How about I walk over there with my glasses on, but then I'll take them off before I speak to him?"

Kit nodded. "I can allow that."

Mae smiled. She straightened her shoulders and turned in Slade's direction. She might have barbecue sauce on her white T-shirt and thick, too-large glasses, but she was going to talk to him come heck or high water.

All her determination vanished as she searched for the spot Slade had been sitting. She felt like she'd been slugged in the gut. Slade was gone.

She ran toward where he'd been, dodging tables and waiters. He'd been gone long enough that the table had been cleared and an older couple was sitting in his vacated spot. No! She pushed through the crowded restaurant and out onto the street. The sun had already sunk to the west and the night was deepening. She squinted around, looking for his tall frame and dark hair. Nothing.

Taking a chance, she ran to the north, praying, hoping she'd find him.

"Mae!" Kit yelled at her from behind. "Where is he?"

"I don't know! Go that direction, please."

"Okay."

Mae jogged around tourists, baby strollers, and families on the sidewalk. She couldn't see him anywhere. Despair crept in. Maybe she was wrong and Slade wasn't her destiny. She'd been so proud of herself for working up the nerve to go talk to him, and everything had gone wrong. Second-guessing going out with him tomorrow, she kept searching the street, but she didn't see him anywhere.

CHAPTER THREE

Slade woke early the next morning and ran from the Four Seasons along the piers and through Presidio Park and Golden Gate Park. It was a nice run, but he couldn't get his mind off his dinner with Mae tonight. He stopped on his way back through Presidio and wandered off the jogging trail and down to the beach, where he pulled his phone out and texted her.

Did you decide where I'm taking you to dinner tonight?

Immediately the dots appeared, showing she was texting. *You claim to be brave enough to eat anything. Can you handle your sushi?*

He smiled. *I can sushi you under the table.*

I'll take that challenge. We'll eat nigiri until your gut bursts.

Sounds perfect. What time and where?

Sushi Sticks. 6. Don't be late or I'll ditch you.

Slade grinned. *I wouldn't dare be late for a dream date like this.*

No dots appeared, and Slade wondered if he'd pushed too hard. Mae was hilarious and confident, but she was obviously hiding behind those glasses and ill-fitting T-shirts and she'd let it slip once that she rarely left Sausalito.

He wandered along the beach, enjoying the sunshine on this spring day and praying he hadn't scared her away—which was silly, because he wasn't looking for anything more than dinner.

Finally, the dots appeared. *I'm so much cooler than your dreams. Prepare for the night of your life, son.*

Slade laughed. He liked her. It was okay to admit that much. It didn't mean he was going to get involved. She lived across the country. She didn't like exposure or media, which were a big part of his life no matter what he wanted. There was no way he would relocate from Lottie and his family in Boston, and Mae didn't seem keen on leaving Sausalito.

He stopped in his tracks and shook his head to clear it. He was racing way ahead of himself, and that was completely unlike him. He was going out to dinner with a fun friend who he enjoyed teasing with. End of story. No worries.

He typed back. *Can't wait.*

Then he forced himself to pocket his phone and jog back to the trail. He needed to put Mae and tonight's dinner from his mind and focus on work. Work was good. Work was familiar.

He smiled as he ran toward his hotel. *I'm so much cooler than your dreams.* He more than liked her.

Mae was in the middle of an excruciating boot camp class at the small gym Kit managed when Slade started texting her. Immediately she ran out of class, ignoring Kit hollering at her, so she could focus on the text stream. She squealed when he called her a dream date.

Then doubts crept in. Who was she kidding? Slade Steele was charming—of course he knew how to flirt with women—but would he lead her on like that? He was also classy and had to know she didn't date men like him. Truth be told, she didn't date at all, and he could probably sense that as well.

When she typed her bold line, *I'm so much cooler than your dreams. Prepare for the night of your life, son,* she was sweating more than she'd ever sweated at the boot camp class. His simple *can't wait* had her panting for air. He couldn't wait. Truly! She was so excited and nervous and … she needed to throw up somewhere. Pacing the front sidewalk, she swallowed back bile and clutched at her stomach. She couldn't do this.

The class filtered out of the gym's front doors a few minutes later. Several people from the class said goodbye to her, and then Kit appeared.

"What are you doing ditching out on burpees?" Kit folded her arms across her trim chest and glared adorably as only Kit could do.

"Slade texted." Mae held her phone aloft.

Kit's teal eyes lit up and she grabbed the phone from Mae's

hand, reading it back and smiling to herself. "You realize you're the cutest person in the whole world, right?"

Mae swallowed down the emotion. "You realize you're the only person who thinks that?"

Kit's mouth dropped open. "That's not true. My parents, brothers, and sisters-in-law all agree, and from these texts, I think Slade agrees also."

"Thanks, Kit. That means a lot, but you're getting way ahead of yourself. Slade's a charming, classy guy. He doesn't mean any of this."

"You don't know that." Kit jutted out a hip, but then her eyes softened. "Mae." She stepped closer and tugged at her ponytail. "Can you do something for me? Best friend asking here."

Mae smiled. "I'd do anything for you."

"Let me make you over today."

Mae's eyes widened, and she stepped back. She hadn't even thought of that.

"You're hiding behind the glasses, the no makeup or hair done, the frumpy clothes. Please, Mae. Is Slade Steele your dream man, or have you just talked about him nonstop for years to make me crazy?"

Mae bit at her lip and finally admitted, "I love him. Well, you know I don't truly love him, but I love everything about him." She truly loved him, but she didn't need to look completely pathetic, even to the person she trusted more than any other.

"Let's do this, then. Stop hiding. You're an absolute angel inside and out. I am certain Slade knows and appreciates your adorable insides; let him have the complete package. For me."

Mae's stomach filled with ice. "But Kit ... Even if you dolled me up as fakey as you could get me, I wouldn't be worthy of Slade. I'd never fit in his world."

"You're wrong. You're out of *his* league. Nobody deserves you, Mae, but I also think you have some illusion about what world Slade lives in. I've dated men like him, and they're great. They're fun to be around, charismatic, kind. Yes, they are more driven, successful, and influential than the average person, but Slade would never make you feel like a lower-class citizen. Don't let yourself feel that way. Savvy?"

Mae got all choked up at her friend's words, and people were pulling into the parking lot for Kit's next class. She gave her friend a quick, sweaty hug—gross, but needed—and muttered, "Savvy. Let's do it."

"Yes!" Kit squealed, squeezed her tighter, and lifted her off her feet. Plopping her back down, she punched both fists in the air. "Yeah, baby! My girl is going to slay Slade Steele!"

A woman walking into the gym stopped and stared at Mae as if she were an alien. "Truly? *You're* going after Slade Steele? As in the Patriots superstar Preston Steele's brother? Slade's the super wealthy, good-looking one, right?"

Mae's stomach churned. Kit's pep talk aside, she wasn't in Slade's social class, nor was she in Slade's beauty class.

"Slade's going after *her*," Kit said, giving the lady a challenging glare.

The woman's jaw dropped. "Wow. Changing up his MO."

"Go get warmed up," Kit commanded the lady.

The woman shrugged and walked inside.

Kit glared after her. "She's going to be dripping with sweat and begging for mercy after this class. What a brat."

Mae swallowed. The lady's tone of voice hadn't been bratty. She'd been truly shocked. She blew out a breath and mumbled, "I need to get some work done."

Kit nodded. "Okay. I'm done with classes and training at one. I'll make appointments and pick you up at one-thirty."

"Thanks." Mae wandered toward the bike rack. Would a makeover even matter? You couldn't change a leopard's spots, no matter how badly you wanted to.

CHAPTER FOUR

The beauty salon had been an insane experience for Mae. Kit was a woman on a mission, and she'd had several people working on Mae at the same time. One lady was putting on fake eyelashes while another was manicuring her fingernails. Another lady was highlighting her hair while yet another worked on her makeup. It was absolutely insane, but she'd survived. Kit had even gotten ahold of their family friend and eye doctor and picked up some contact samples. Mae had been surprised how comfortable the contacts felt. She'd hidden behind her glasses, assuming they were easier to use. Looking around at the bright world outside the large windows of her home, she felt like she could finally see, not impaired by her glasses' frames or weight.

Kit burst in the front door, her arms laden with dresses and shoes. "Okay, we've only got twenty minutes before I need to drive you to Sushi Sticks."

"I can walk. It's like half a mile away." Mae walked or biked everywhere. Occasionally, if emergency necessitated it, she used an Uber or Lyft.

Kit's jaw dropped. "You are not walking in these heels! I had to borrow them from my mom because your foot's smaller than mine. I wish we'd had more time to go into the city and shop, but the ferry takes too long."

Mae's stomach tightened. Kit knew what the city and driving across the Golden Gate Bridge did to her. The few times Kit or her family had gotten Mae into the city, they'd been understanding and took the ferry or rented a boat to get across the bay. They were truly the best people.

"Thanks for sharing your clothes and your mom's shoes," Mae said, hoping they could avoid dissecting the emotional damage from her past right now. She wanted to be upbeat and happy for her date with Slade.

"Of course. Mom was thrilled about it and only asked for pictures and details later. You're going to look so fabulous." Kit strode toward the stairs and Mae's upstairs bedroom. She'd had her parents' home redone when she got her first bonus from Slade's company, but she couldn't bring herself to touch her parents' or sisters' bedrooms. Instead, she'd shut those rooms off, turning her room and the guest bedroom and bath upstairs into a suite that overlooked the bay. She loved it.

They ascended the stairs, and Kit dropped her load of dresses and shoes on the bed. She shoved a light-blue slinky dress at her first. "Try this one. I think it'll be perfect."

Mae's stomach squirmed. Would Slade be all dressed up? What if she was overdressed and he realized how desperately she wanted him and how awkward she was? "What if he's not dressed up?"

"Have you never Googled the man?"

"Only three to four times a day."

"Did you see him last night?"

"Not very clearly. Someone stole my glasses."

Kit laughed. "True that. Sorry, sis. Well, he looked fabulous, and he was wearing an open-collared button-down shirt with slacks, but no tie. You told me he'd just flown in, so obviously he dresses nice most of the time. Plus, he's excited about this date. He'll be dressed up."

Mae bit at her lip. She highly doubted Slade was excited about this date or thought much of it. His texts were probably teasing, as usual.

"Stop biting off your lipstick." Kit pushed the dress against her chest. "You're going to look fabulous. Try it on!"

Mae walked into her attached bathroom, flicking the light on. She stopped and stared at herself in the mirror. She'd almost forgotten that the contacts weren't the only transformation. She had makeup on and her dark hair had beautiful golden highlights added to it. Her hair was in long curls, and with the tastefully done eyelashes and her full lips a beautiful pink, she had to admit she looked like a woman off the movie screen. Maybe Slade would think she was beautiful and want to date her.

She slipped out of her T-shirt and shorts and into the dress quickly. Its capped sleeves showed off her toned shoulders and arms, its knee-length hemline was classy but displayed her lean calf muscles, and it molded to her body perfectly. The pale blue sort of shimmered and made her skin and dark eyes look amazing. She squealed just like Kit would. "I love it!"

Kit yanked the door open. Mae spun, and her friend's face was all the confirmation she needed. "Yes! I'm a genius and you are gorgeous. Yes!" Kit pulled her out into the bedroom and grabbed some sparkly silver heels off the bed. "Try these."

Mae slid them on, teetering, and stood almost as tall as Kit's five-eight. "I'm going to trip and fall on these."

"We've got a few minutes to practice."

Mae held on to Kit's arm, and they walked around the room several times. Then Kit got her a silver purse ready with lip gloss, her phone, and a credit card. They descended the stairs and Mae was wobbly, but she miraculously didn't fall. She went solo across the living room and out the front door, only teetering a few times.

"You got this. Dang, your calves look goo-ood. I rock as a fitness trainer, don't I?"

"Yes, your morning torture is finally worth it. Maybe burpees aren't a complete waste." Mae didn't point out that walking and biking everywhere might have contributed to the striations in her calves.

Kit held the car door for her, glowering. "It's fun, not torture, and we work hard for optimal health, not just to look good."

Mae laughed. "Keep telling yourself that."

Kit grinned, slammed her door, then hurried around to get in. "And we're off to our dream date!"

They drove quickly to the restaurant. Mae's palms were sweating, and she almost wiped them on her dress, but she caught herself. "Sorry," she mumbled, seeing Kit's chagrined look.

"You're okay, sweetie. You're absolutely amazing, and he's going to love you."

"Thanks," Mae forced out, not really believing the pep talk.

"But if you ruin my dress with sweat, I'm going to take it out of your hide at the gym in the morning."

Mae did an exaggerated full-body shiver. "I'll be good, I promise."

Kit laughed as she pulled up to the front door of the sushi place and slammed it into park. She looked over and dabbed dramatically at her eyes. "I feel like a proud mama."

"Thanks, Kit ... for everything."

"Of course." Kit squeezed her hand. Mae pulled on the door handle, but Kit didn't let go. "Wait! Prayer."

"Thank you again." Mae released her pent-up breath.

Kit said a short prayer for Mae to be calm, to be herself, and to have a wonderful and safe evening. They squeezed hands again, Mae mumbled one more thank-you, and then she was on the sidewalk, looking at the sushi restaurant's front doors and trembling from head to foot.

"The prayer didn't work," she muttered to herself, but then she felt instant guilt. She needed to have faith. She said another silent prayer, threw her shoulders back, and strutted toward the restaurant. Tripping on who knew what, she fell forward and smacked her shoulder on the door. "Ouch!" she yelped.

Clinging to the door handle, she glanced back to see Kit leaning across the car console with the passenger-side window down. "You okay, sweetie?"

"Doing fantabulous. Good thing we got the contacts, though. Can you imagine how bad this would be with me blind?"

"Worse than last night." Kit blew her a kiss.

The restaurant door swung open. Mae stepped back, teetering but luckily not falling. Two men came out, looked her up and down, and smiled appreciatively. One held the door.

"Thank you," Mae murmured.

"Are you alone?" he rushed out.

"Meeting someone."

He nodded, his eyes dimming. "Have a great night."

"You too."

She walked in, and the hostess smiled at her. "For one?"

Mae felt like her tongue was stuck to the roof of her mouth. "I'm ... meeting someone. Can I sit at a corner table until my friend gets here?"

"Of course." The hostess led the way to a table where Mae would have a view of the entire restaurant, and Mae luckily didn't fall in the heels.

She sat down, and a male waiter brought her a water and set a menu down. "Anything to drink besides water?"

"No thank you. I'm waiting for someone."

"All right." He grinned at her. He had a great smile, and the confident and appealing way he carried himself made her feel comfortable around him. "I'll be back to check on you in a minute."

"Thank you." Mae realized she was clinging to the clutch purse thing. She set it on the table and tried to appear relaxed and charming. She crossed her legs, put a smile on her face, and put her shoulders back. Seconds ticked by as long as hours, and she waited and waited, staring at the entrance to the restaurant and praying furiously. *Please let him come. Please let him like me.*

The waiter came back. "Are you still doing all right? Can I start you an appetizer? Maybe a daiquiri, Diet Coke, or flavored lemonade?"

Mae blinked furiously. Something about the Diet Coke made her flash back to yesterday. She had been wearing her Diet Coke shirt and trying to get to Slade, and it didn't work. Were they not meant to meet? Was he ditching her? How many minutes must have passed for the waiter to be checking back in with her? "I'm fine, really. Thank you." She blinked and blinked, but a tear spilled out. She gasped. Kit would kill her for ruining this makeup.

The waiter's bright blue eyes widened. He whipped a napkin

from the silverware, squatted down in front of her, and gently blotted the tear on her face. "Is he someone important to you?" he asked quietly.

Mae nodded, unable to speak. She really appreciated his kindness.

"If he stands you up, he's the biggest idiot on the planet."

"Thank you," she managed.

He nodded and stood. "And just for the record, it's not just because of how beautiful you are. You have a light that shines from you. It's more than obvious that you're as pretty on the inside."

Mae put a hand to her heart. "Thank you again."

He smiled. "And if he doesn't show up, I'll find a replacement to work for me and I'll take you out. If you're interested."

Mae laughed, tears forgotten for the moment. Anyone would be interested in this handsome and kind man, but she wanted Slade. "I have a beautiful friend I'll set you up with."

He smiled and turned away, but not before she heard him mutter, "Sweetheart, no friend could compare to you."

Mae sat there, stunned. She hadn't had attention from men in so long that she'd forgotten how wonderful it felt. The waiter left, and she kept perusing the restaurant. Would Slade really stand her up? Then a horrific thought hit her. The Golden Gate Bridge! Supposedly, the accident and fatality rate on the bridge was lower than most, but she didn't believe it. That bridge had already stolen most of the people she loved. What if Slade had gotten in an accident?

Her body went cold and her head was too big for her shoulders. Not Slade. She had no claim on the man and no relationship with him, but she already loved him. What could she do?

She heard her phone ding with an incoming text. Ripping the purse open, she pulled the phone out with trembling fingers.

Accident on the bridge. My driver says at least twenty minutes. So sorry I'm late.

Mae felt the anxiety leave her. She said a prayer for whoever was in the accident, thankful it wasn't Slade. He hadn't ditched her, and he wasn't dead, and the waiter had said she was beautiful. Slade would come, and this night could still be the best of her life. It would just start a little later.

I told you not to be late. She included a laughing emoji so he'd know she was teasing.

Believe me, I would swim to you if I could.

Mae grinned. How cute was he? *But then you'd smell like seaweed and lose all chance of a goodnight kiss.* She hit send, but she was horrified when she realized what she'd said. Slade probably thought of her as a work associate or a buddy. Between the waiter tonight, Mike hitting on her yesterday, and being dolled up, she'd built up too much confidence. She was making a complete fool of herself with Slade. She waited with bated breath as he typed.

Good thing I'm wearing my Armani Code, then, isn't it?

Mae bit at her lip and held in a squeal, but only because the restaurant was crowded. It was highly possible he was simply teasing with her. They teased each other all the time, so that was the likeliest scenario, but she could still hope. *Very good thing.*

Please order some appetizers and a drink for you. I hate the thought of you sitting there with no man and no food.

Oh my, how she loved him. Was it really possible Slade could be interested in someone like her? Not the her sitting here all dolled up, but the her that wore baggy T-shirts and huge glasses and had issues nobody should have to deal with because of her family's deaths.

I can do that. She typed. *Get here safe.*

I can do that. See you soon.

Mae stowed her phone in her purse, grinning like a fool.

"With a smile like that, I'd say he's at least on his way." The waiter had approached from the side.

"Realized he didn't want to miss out on all this fun." She gave a confident wink she wasn't feeling.

"He's a very lucky man." The waiter grinned. "Would you like anything while you wait?"

"He told me to order some appetizers. Would you bring some veggie tempura and some yellow-tail nigiri? Oh, and I'd love that Diet Coke you offered earlier."

"Of course, my lady. Coming right up." He bowed slightly and walked away.

Mae relaxed in her chair, finally not apprehensive or scared. Slade seemed to be genuinely interested in her. Even if it wasn't romantic, he would never be degrading or mean to her. Would he like the way she looked tonight? Would being here together, with her making an effort to be attractive for him, change their relationship? Happy bubbles filled her stomach. It was exciting and fun, and the possibilities opening up were more exhilarating than anything she'd experienced in her short, boring life.

She smiled at other people in the restaurant, people-watching for a while. The friendly waiter brought her Diet Coke and the appetizers. He was extremely handsome, but she wasn't interested in anyone but Slade.

She picked at the food but couldn't eat much with the happy nerves surging through her. Twenty minutes passed, and she was watching the entryway diligently again. Any minute now, he was going to walk around the fancy barrier that gave separation to the entryway. She reapplied the fancy gloss coating that was supposed to go over her lipstick, rubbed some coconut and lime-scented lotion into her hands and discreetly on her neck, and studied the spot where he should appear.

Slade strode around the barrier, and her heart stopped. He looked better than she could've imagined. He was in a white button-down shirt that was open at the collar, a navy suit coat, and gray slacks. His face was sculpted and manly, and his dark eyes with those darker lashes about killed her. He moistened his well-formed lips and his eyes perused the restaurant.

His gaze stopped on her and lit with interest.

Mae smiled invitingly, her heart walloping against her chest and her every dream about to come true. Should she stand, wave, go give him a hug? Was a kiss permissible yet? What about touching his chest? No, she needed to stop those thoughts, pray to have a magical evening with Slade, and then pray harder that he went for a kiss. Tonight was going to change her entire life. She felt it.

Slade nodded slightly to her, and then his eyes continued to peruse the crowded restaurant.

What the ... what? Mae blinked, confused and suddenly scared. Was Slade looking for someone else? Was she not attractive to him all dolled up? What if he didn't even recognize her? She started second-guessing everything about herself and her makeover. If she went and rubbed off all her makeup and put one of her funny T-shirts on, would Slade smile at her?

Slade kept glancing around and around, and then his face drooped. He chatted with the hostess briefly, and she led him to a two-person table across the restaurant from where Mae was sitting. What had just happened? Why wasn't he coming to her?

Her phone buzzed, finally breaking her concentration on Slade, and she picked it up with clammy fingers.

Did you give up on me? I'm so sorry I'm late.

Give up on him? He hadn't recognized her. So many weird emotions were rolling through her. What should she say? What should she do? All her insecurities and fears surfaced, and all she wanted to do was run and hide with a Diet Coke and her friends Ghirardelli, Lindt, and Cadbury. How could Slade not know her? She didn't know how to respond, but she finally texted: *I had to run. Sorry. Maybe we'll make it happen next time you're in town.*

Mae bit at her lip, then remembered that Kit would be ticked if she messed up her makeup. She was more worried that she was letting her self-doubt rule her. She was messing up the entire night. Yet something inside had shriveled when he hadn't recognized her. She snuck a glance across the restaurant, but his head was bowed over his phone and she couldn't see his expression. Something in the defeated round of his shoulders made her want to rush over and hug him, but she was frozen to her chair.

Finally, the dots appeared. *I can't pretend I'm not disappointed. I can wait if there's any way you can make time to meet me tonight.*

Oh, man. That was sweet of him. He really wanted to meet her. Mae sat there, debating. What should she do?

"Is he still coming, or is it time for me to find a work replacement so I can officially ask you out?"

Mae glanced up at the waiter. She didn't know what to say.

"Is he going to make you cry again? I'm really starting to hate this guy."

Mae smiled. "I don't know what to think. He came, but ... he didn't recognize me."

"Excuse me?"

"We've only done video chats." She shook her head. "But it hurts, you know? Why wouldn't he recognize me?"

The guy nodded. "I can see why that would hurt. What are you going to do?"

"I told him I had to leave because he was late. Was that wrong?"

"I kind of feel like he had it coming."

Mae shrugged. "I don't know about that, but it's … we don't have a relationship, but I'm head over heels for him, and now he didn't even recognize me. Honestly, I'm thinking I should have you go over and tell him this dolled-up version of me wants to have dinner with him. See if he's even committed to the real me, or if he'd go for the pretty girl because he thinks I left. Does that make any sense?"

He tilted his head. "Do you not usually dress up? Is that why he didn't recognize you?"

She nodded miserably.

"Hmm. It could be fun. So we'll see if he'll have dinner with this 'dolled-up version' of you. If he refuses the offer, then you'll know he's fully invested in the real you and might even be worthy of you." He gave her a kind smile. "Then I'll tell him your real name, and he gets the prize of dinner with you. If he takes the … not real you up on your offer to have dinner together, and especially if he hits on you, not knowing it's you, then he's not worthy of you and you'll at least give me a chance."

"So, we give him a test? That's what the riddle we both keep spinning means, right?"

He laughed. "Yep. A test it is. And I'm praying he fails so I get the chance to officially ask you out."

That was really kind of the waiter, but Mae was praying Slade passed. She thought it was a good test. If Slade would come eat with her, flirt, and even kiss someone he'd just met, then all of Mae's inflated hopes were stupid. All her dreams were one-sided.

She realized they didn't have a relationship, so it wouldn't be wrong of Slade to take someone else up on a dinner offer, but she could prevent a lot of heartache for herself by finding out what he'd do with the offer. "Okay, let's do it. Tell him my name is ... Josie. Tell him my date couldn't come and I'd love to not eat alone."

"Okay." He winked. "Here's to him failing."

Mae laughed, but she was wringing her hands together as he walked away. *Please don't let him fail. Please don't let him fail.*

CHAPTER FIVE

Slade rushed into the restaurant thirty-five minutes late, praying that she hadn't given up on him. There was just something about Mae, and he really wanted this chance to spend time with her in person. He needed to see if their friendship had the possibility of more.

He glanced around the restaurant, his eyes landing on an absolutely exquisite brunette. For a brief second, he thought he'd just seen the woman of his dreams. He tried to tell himself he was acting shallow and only basing that on outside looks. Yet there was light, intelligence, and humor that shone from her beautiful deep brown eyes that said she was much more than her perfect exterior.

No ... He blinked as if coming out of a daze. He wasn't going to check out another woman when he'd asked Mae out, no matter how intrigued he was by the woman. He nodded to the beauty and kept searching for Mae. His shoulders felt heavy as he realized she wasn't anywhere in the restaurant. He'd really been looking forward to spending time with her. The hostess escorted him to a table, and he texted Mae.

Did you give up on me? I'm so sorry I'm late. He waited impatiently, hoping she was just in the restroom.

I had to run. Sorry. Maybe we'll make it happen next time you're in town.

Disappointment ripped through him. She'd left. Shoot. *I can't pretend I'm not disappointed. I can wait if there's any way you can make time to meet me tonight.*

Slade waited and waited. His gut churned as the seconds ticked by and no response came. Frustrated, he wondered if he should've left the San Francisco offices earlier. Yet it wasn't his fault there was a wreck on the bridge. He and Mae had developed a friendship over the years, and now, when he was going to finally spend some time with her in person, she'd ditched him.

The waiter approached him. Slade forced a smile.

"Hey, man," the waiter said.

"How's it going?" Slade asked.

"I think it's going better for you than for me."

"I doubt that."

The waiter raised an eyebrow. His blue eyes had an appraising look in them. "You see the woman sitting alone?" He gestured his head across the restaurant to the brunette Slade had noticed as he walked in. She glanced at them, then quickly looked away.

She seemed almost unsure of herself or shy, which made no sense with as stunning as she was.

Slade nodded.

"Her date's not coming, and you're the luckiest guy I know. She wants to eat dinner with you."

Slade studied the woman, wondering how her long, shiny hair or the smooth curve of her jaw would feel under his fingertips. It was hard to say no to such an appealing beauty, especially with the instant connection he'd felt to her, but he felt like he'd be betraying Mae if he went over and met his dream woman. Yet it wasn't like he and Mae were even dating, and that woman was more enticing than anyone he'd noticed in a long, long time.

He debated a few more seconds then shook his head. "Will you please tell her thank you for the compliment, but I'm meeting someone?" His shoulders lowered. "Or at least I was."

The guy arched an eyebrow. "So, are you meeting someone, or aren't you?"

Slade glanced at his phone. No new messages. Nothing from Mae. He was surprised how disappointed he felt. He and Mae were only friends, business associates, but he'd really wanted to meet her in person and spend some time with her. "I guess she isn't coming," he muttered.

"So, your date isn't coming and you're turning down the opportunity to eat dinner with a woman as incredible as that one? I can promise you that if I wasn't working, I'd be begging her to go out."

"What's her name?" Slade asked. He needed time to think.

There was nothing wrong with eating dinner with a beautiful woman, but he was still wrapping his mind around the lost opportunity of being with Mae.

"Josie."

"Hmm," he grunted. He really wanted to be with the funny and intriguing Mae tonight, but she'd ditched him. He'd eaten alone last night, and he hadn't minded it, but it would be nice to have someone to talk to, take the sting out of Mae ditching him. Was it going to be awkward the next time they video chatted for work?

Josie glanced over at them, and something in her dark gaze tugged at Slade. She appeared uncertain and vulnerable, which was surprising for a woman that perfect-looking. It made her even more fascinating.

"Come on, man. How could you turn her down? It's just dinner."

Slade knew the waiter was right. He was making the situation too complicated. It *was* just dinner, Mae had left, and Josie was more than another pretty face; he felt like he was being tugged by invisible tendrils from across the restaurant.

He stood and extended his hand. The waiter took it, and they shook. "Thanks. Slade Steele."

"Dirk Miller."

"Nice to meet you." The guy seemed familiar to him, but he couldn't quite place why. "Do I know you?"

"Nah." Dirk clapped him on the shoulder. "Enjoy your dinner."

"Thanks."

The waiter gave him a thumbs-up and stepped back, something glinting in his blue eyes that Slade didn't like. It was almost like the guy was setting him up, but Slade didn't really care. He'd already been ditched by the woman he wanted to be with. If the brunette beauty didn't turn out to be as incredible as she appeared, it was no sweat off his back. It only meant that his intuition was off.

Slade strode across the restaurant. As he approached her table, Josie turned to him. Her deep brown eyes widened. She stood quickly and faced him. Slade stuttered to a stop and his mouth went dry. He'd been around many beautiful women, but everything about this woman was simply perfect—long, dark hair with golden highlights; flawless skin, large eyes, and full lips; and a fit body encased in a pale blue dress that showed off her smooth, tanned skin.

"Hi," he managed to get out.

Her lovely mouth turned down and she clung to the chair. "You failed," she muttered.

"Excuse me?"

Shaking her head, her long, silky hair brushed across her shoulders, and he had the insane urge to see how both felt under his fingertips. "I thought you were ..." She swallowed. "Someone different." Releasing the chair, she turned and hurried toward the exterior exit. She didn't move quickly, as it was obvious she wasn't comfortable in her three-inch heels.

Slade stared after her, confused and more certain that the waiter had set him up. He turned, and the guy was watching him with a smirk. Slade raised his hands in confusion.

"Go after her," the waiter mouthed.

Slade was about sick of taking that guy's advice, but he didn't want her to leave like that. Throwing down a couple twenty-dollar bills on her table, he hurried around the barrier and saw her pushing through the door and heading outside, talking on her phone. He had no clue what was going on, but he was almost as frustrated as he had been when Mae ditched him. Women didn't just walk away from him. He needed some answers, and maybe the chance to touch her hair and shoulders.

CHAPTER SIX

Mae pushed through the exterior door as Kit answered the phone.

"Why are you calling me?" Kit demanded. "You should be with Slade."

"It all went wrong," Mae got out, her voice trembling. "He was late, then he didn't even recognize me, then he failed the test."

"What? What test?"

Mae walked with mincing steps along the sidewalk, wanting to put distance between her and Slade and the mess in the restaurant. She probably should've taken the good-looking waiter up on his offer to go out, but that would make her no better than Slade, just wanting the next hot date. Yet was that really true? Slade had always seemed so genuine to her, and she knew the real reason she'd never date the handsome waiter was because she only wanted Slade. Why, then, had she freaked out and acted so weird when Slade came over? Being in that close of proximity to him had fried her brain. He'd said his cologne was Armani Code. It was delectable, like a sexy man sitting by a warm fire on a winter's night. What she wouldn't give to hold Slade close in front of a fire.

"Too much to explain," she told Kit, "but basically, he thinks I'm some girl named Josie and I just made a fool of myself and walked out on him and ... Oh, Kit, why didn't he even recognize me?"

"Well, the Coke bottle glasses that usually cover half of your face might be the root of the problem. Go back in there and tell him who you are!"

"No, I can't. He'll think I'm insane."

"Then go back in there, pretend to be Josie, and have a great date with him."

"But I want him to love me as Mae." She felt whiny, confused, and so miserable.

"Josie? Josie?" someone called from a few feet behind her.

Mae froze. "He's coming after me," she gritted out.

"Yes! Yes! I told you, you were irresistibly gorgeous. Pretend to be Josie or tell him the truth. Either way, I want you to make out with that man tonight. Love ya!" Kit hung up.

Mae heard his strong, sure footsteps as he approached. She slid the phone back into her purse and slung the purse over her shoulder, but she didn't turn around. The water from the bay gently lapped onto the ground ten feet away. A car drove by.

People's voices carried from the open-air restaurant across the street. All she could concentrate on was Steele Slade standing right behind her, and she couldn't get her body to cooperate and turn around.

"Josie?"

Oh shoot, he'd called her Josie. He thought she was somebody else completely. Mae wanted to correct him, but she wasn't brave enough.

He slowly walked around her on the sidewalk until he was standing right in front of her. He didn't get in her space, but he was close enough she could appreciate all his gloriousness. Even though she was wearing her heels, he was much taller than her. He exuded confidence, manliness, and charm, and he hadn't even said anything. She put a hand to her heart. Oh man, she was in trouble.

"Are you okay?" His rich voice was so familiar from all their chats, but hearing it in person gave it a depth that made her stomach quiver.

She wanted to ease in close and touch him. Slade was finally here, right in front of her, but because she was socially stunted she'd messed it all up, and now he would think she was insane. She took a step back, and his dark gaze got even more serious. She was used to Slade laughing or smiling at things she said. She didn't like seeing him serious and almost sad.

"I'm sorry," she muttered. "This night has not gone anything like it should."

He nodded. "Tell me about it."

Mae tilted her head to the side. "Was that a serious 'tell me about it' like you actually care about my ruined night, or a sarcastic 'tell me about it' as in your failed night is worse than mine and you can commiserate?"

Slade smiled, and everything was suddenly all right again. She'd made him smile in real life and without him even knowing who she was. Now if she could only touch him, she could live in her daydreams of tonight's experience the rest of her life.

Actually, that might be exactly what she should do: flirt, have fun, and kiss this perfect specimen. There was no world where Slade Steele would be interested in frumpy Mae Delaney, but he was obviously interested in Josie ... whatever her lame last name was. Why not enjoy it? Tomorrow morning and her reclusive, sad life would come soon enough.

"Truthfully, a little of both," he said. "I am interested in why your night is a failure and my night did not go anywhere according to plan, so I can definitely 'commiserate.'"

She smiled. Why did she have to like him so much?

"Do you want to tell me about it?" he asked.

She shrugged. "Same old story, actually. Girl loves boy, but he's out of her league."

Slade held up a hand. "Excuse me, I have to stop you right there. No man could possibly be out of your league."

Did he truly mean that? Tingles erupted on her skin but she was even more confused. He meant Josie, not Mae, right? Gesturing to her perfectly made-up self, she asked quietly, "Because of this?"

He appraised her and arched an eyebrow. "I won't lie and say you aren't the most gorgeous woman I've ever seen ..."

Mae swallowed hard and almost fell off her borrowed three-inch heels. Would Slade hand out inflated praise like Tic Tacs? That didn't seem like him, but what did she really know about him besides their video chats for work and what the media portrayed? Yet her chest warmed with his kind words. Could he truly think the made-up Mae was the most gorgeous woman he'd ever seen?

"But it's more than that." He took a step closer, and she was overwhelmed by that glorious amber-scented cologne. "There are so many things shining from your eyes. Intelligence, humor, and light. I can tell that you're kind and funny. There's also a sweetness and humility about you that I've rarely seen in a woman as incredibly beautiful as you."

Mae couldn't have spoken if she wanted to. Slade really saw all that from a few glances and a short conversation? Yet he was saying all of this to Josie, not to her. Or was he saying it to Mae? She was so confused right now.

He gave a forced smile. "I've revealed too much. My sister would say I don't know how to play hard to get."

"Why would you ever have to play any games?"

"What do you mean?"

"You're ... perfect." She admitted, gesturing to him. "Any woman would want to date you."

"Would you?" He cocked a challenging eyebrow.

"I ... um ..." She fumbled for words. She would die to date him as Mae, but she didn't want to date him under these misguided intentions.

"I forget myself. You were waiting for someone else, and you obviously want to be with him. What's he like?"

Mae studied Slade for a few seconds. "He's funny, smart, kind, handsome, perfect to me."

Slade's dark eyes reflected pain. "He's a lucky man."

"He would be if he showed up." She winked.

Slade laughed. "He's a fool to not show up."

"Thank you." Rather than risk throwing herself at him, she stored his words to savor later, then asked, "What about you? Why is your night failed?"

"Would you like to walk for a while?"

"Sure." Spending more time with him, even under a presumed identity, wasn't something she could turn down.

He turned, and she started forward on the thankfully quiet side-walk. Cars were still driving slowly past and the restaurants were crowded on this beautiful early summer night, but it felt like they were almost alone. Mae cursed her inability to walk in these shoes. She had to move slowly, but Slade didn't seem to mind and fell into measured steps next to her.

"So why is your night failed?" she asked again. She didn't dare look at him for fear she'd trip and fall.

"I was supposed to have dinner with a lady I've known for a couple of years but have never met in person."

"Were you excited to meet her?" She risked a glance at him, and he was smiling to himself.

"Yeah. She's really funny and smart, and I like the way she makes me feel."

Mae's heart was walloping against her chest. *Tell him who you are!* a voice screamed in her mind, but her tongue wouldn't cooperate.

"Sorry." He caught her looking at him and appeared chagrined. "That's really classless of me to talk about another woman while I'm walking with you."

She smiled. "I did the same thing to you earlier, and I like hearing about her. What's her name?"

"Mae." He tilted his head to study her. "You remind me of her."

Mae's heart was racing so fast she'd probably need a defibrillator to reregulate it. "I'll take that as the highest compliment," she said.

"You should. She's an amazing lady."

Mae grinned and bit at her lip. He really seemed to like her, both the fake her and the real her. Was it even possible?

They walked for a while in silence before Slade spoke again. "It's odd because I have no relationship with her, and honestly she isn't the type of woman I usually date, but ... there's something about Mae that I can't get out of my mind. Again, I apologize. It's wrong to talk about her when I'm with you. There's something about you that makes me want to share all my secrets." He grinned. "You probably get that a lot."

"Oh, yeah," she said wryly. "Men just want to share all about other women when they're with me."

He chuckled. "I didn't mean it like that. I'm sure most men have a hard time remembering there are other women in existence when they're around you." He glanced at her and kept walking slowly. "I've rarely seen such beauty as yours. You sparkle."

Mae's brain was spinning. In one breath he was saying he couldn't get Mae out of his mind, and in the next he was complimenting Josie. She was confused and happy and wanted to kiss him so badly right now. What would he do if she just touched him? Her body felt drawn to his. He had a magnetic pull she didn't think she could resist much longer. If she could just get one small touch, maybe his hand or his arm, it would satiate her in the long, lonely Slade-free years to come. She couldn't let herself dream of a relationship with this perfect man, and after being close to him, no one else would ever do. But there was no way she could admit to Slade that she'd pretended to be someone she wasn't. Especially since he'd said nice things about Mae to Josie. She wasn't even sure who she was right now.

"I shouldn't be complimenting you when I'm supposed to be with someone else," Slade said ruefully, "and here you are, wishing you were with the man who's perfect to you."

Dang, he was a good listener. She didn't mean to push him away, but she couldn't tell him now that he was the guy she'd described.

He pushed a hand through his dark hair. "We're both just a mess, aren't we?"

Her thoughts exactly. "A couple of 'poor, unfortunate souls,'" she sang out.

Slade stopped walking and turned quickly to her. "*Little Mermaid*," he said. "One of my sister Lottie's favorites."

Mae loved that he'd recognized the song. If she sang "Kiss the Girl," would he comply? She turned to him, but her heel caught on a crack or something in the sidewalk. She slammed against his chest. Reaching out to steady herself, her hands ended up on his muscular shoulders. They felt more perfect and manly than she could've imagined.

Slade reacted quickly, his hands wrapping around her waist to steady her. Explosions seemed to go off in her body at his simple touch. His eyes widened as if he felt the exact same way. Throwing sane reactions to the wind, Mae slid her arms around to his upper back and pulled her body flush to his.

Slade looked almost in shock, but his hands moved slowly around to her lower back and he cradled her in close. Mae stared up at his handsome face, and he stared down at her as if she were as intriguing and beautiful as he had claimed earlier. She'd had no clue being held by a man could feel like this. Warm tremors raced through her, and she wanted to stay close to him from now until the end of time.

It was sheer reaction to the tender feelings she'd never experienced anywhere but in novels when she pulled his head down and arched as high as she could on these vicious heels. Slade bowed his head to hers, and their lips met. At first the kiss was soft, tender, and as beautiful as new life. Then Slade let out a quiet moan, his hands tightened around her back, and he pulled her so close she couldn't breathe, and she didn't care to.

She gasped, and he smiled against her lips, then proceeded to kiss her like they'd been designed to fit together. They tasted, they savored, they got so entangled in each other that nothing else in the world mattered to her.

Time stood still, yet it flew by much too quickly. Mae's hands came around to frame his perfect face, and Slade lifted her clean off the ground. He devoured her mouth, and she realized that the books she'd read and the movies she'd watched did not do kissing justice. No imitation could be as unreal and fabulous as kissing Slade.

As his smell and body wrapped around her and his lips took command of her world, Mae knew she'd never be the same. How could she go back to her dull life after this explosion of color, sensation, and joy?

Slade gently set her back on her feet and trailed kisses up her jawline. She shivered from the incredible thrill. She wanted to tell him exactly who she was and go snuggle on her couch, kissing and talking the night away. Slade was the man of her dreams and more. His kiss told her he returned her feelings and then some.

His lips reached her ear and he said in a soft growl, "Mae."

Mae's eyes flew open and she released his face. He knew. Somehow, he knew. She was relieved and happy and yet embarrassed all at the same time.

Slade's eyes also popped open, but they were filled with ... horror. Why was he looking at her like that? He released her so quickly that she teetered on her heels, but miraculously she didn't fall.

Slade backed up a step, staring at her as if he had no clue who she was or what he'd just done. "Josie ... I am so sorry."

Josie? Oh my goodness, he thought she was Josie now? She was as baffled as a pig at the prom.

"I lost my head when you touched me, then I kissed you like that and you returned it ... I shouldn't have called you Mae. I am so sorry."

Mae could only stare at him, confusion and desire for him warring within her. Finally, she squeaked out, "Why did you call me Mae?" *Please let him figure it out,* she prayed. *Let him say he loves me.*

He pushed a hand through his hair. "I have no idea. I've been thinking about her, and then you ... You're irresistible. I've never —" He glanced away and licked his lips. "Never felt that way when I touched or kissed someone before."

Mae's heart gave a leap of joy. This was happening. She was special to Slade, and even though he thought he'd kissed Josie, he'd been thinking of Mae. Could he be any more perfect? She didn't know what to say, where to start.

"Again, I apologize. I would never take advantage of someone like that. I'm confused, and I was in the wrong. Please forgive me." Slade looked so out of sorts she wanted to comfort him, right after she told him who she was and kissed him again.

A taxi pulled up down the street in front of a restaurant. Slade lifted his hand and flagged it. Mae was confused again. Who was he getting a taxi for? Did he want to go somewhere more comfortable so they could talk ... and kiss some more?

The sedan pulled up to them, and Slade yanked open the back door and shoved a couple of twenty-dollar bills at the driver. "Please take her wherever she wants to go."

"Sure, man."

He held the door for her and stepped back. "I am so sorry, Josie. I wish I could pursue this unreal connection between us, but I don't feel right about it. Especially after I kissed you and then called you Mae. I apologize."

Mae had no clue what to say, how to react. She slid into the car and stared up at him, wishing she could say something to clear up this disaster. He gave her a forced smile and shut the door.

"Where to, ma'am?" the taxi driver asked.

Somehow, she rattled off her address, but her eyes were locked on Slade, who hadn't moved. The car pulled away and Slade lifted a hand in farewell. The torn look on his face about killed her. She should make the car stop, tell him who she was, and then kiss him time and time again. Instead, she craned her neck until she couldn't see him any longer, sank down into the seat, and somehow held the tears in until the driver stopped at her house.

She stumbled out of the car and up the sidewalk. Ripping the heels off, she hurried to unlock her door, slammed it behind her, and then slumped to the wooden floor in the entryway. Tears spilled down her face, ruining Kit's carefully constructed makeup.

Kit! Her best friend could fix this. Yanking the phone from her purse, she pushed Kit's name on the recent caller list.

"Why are you calling me again?" Kit demanded. "You should be with Slade."

"Kit!" she wailed. "I messed it all up. Please come help me."

"Where are you?"

"My house."

"I'm on my way."

Mae dropped the phone back in the purse and banged her head against the door behind her. Messed it all up was putting it mildly. She was socially inept and had ruined her own future. Kit was going to kill her.

CHAPTER SEVEN

Slade watched the taxi pull away, more miserable than he'd ever been. Life had been good to him and his family, and things typically went his way. Not tonight. He should never have chased Josie out of the restaurant. He couldn't believe the surge of feelings that had overwhelmed him when he'd touched her, and those kisses ... wow. Powerful didn't begin to describe Josie's intoxicating kiss. Even her smell had made him think he was on a tropical vacation—lime and coconut. Being with her felt like the best escape he'd had in years.

If only they could've met under different circumstances. He was overwhelmed by the guilt of wanting to be with Mae while he was with Josie and the confusion over being so drawn to both women.

The taxi petered from his sight, and Slade pulled out his phone to text his driver. Once the text went through, he clicked on the text stream with Mae, scrolling back and rereading some of her funny quips. With a pang of sadness, he reached the part where she'd left the restaurant because he was late and then never responded to his plea to meet later.

More guilt rippled through him as he realized that if Mae would've stayed and had dinner with him, he never would've met Josie. He paced along the sidewalk, his mind jumping back to how original, innocent, and beautiful Josie was. It was impossible to forget how it felt to touch her and the kisses they'd shared. He passed a hand over his face. Why had he sent her away in that taxi? She was incredible. He and Mae were not dating, and Mae hadn't even wanted to be with him tonight.

He didn't even know Josie's last name or where she lived. A heavy weight filled his gut. How would he find her again? But he didn't want to find her again, right? He was the one who'd sent her away because he felt guilty for secretly wanting to be with Mae, even though he wanted Josie also, and then he'd called Josie Mae in the heat of the moment of their kiss. He was not a two-timer, never, and though he and Mae weren't dating, he hated himself right now.

His phone beeped an incoming FaceTime. Lottie. His sister was exactly what he needed at the moment.

He answered the call, and just seeing her cute face made him feel better. Lottie was sixteen, ten years younger than the youngest of the four Steele brothers, Gunner. The boys were all eighteen months apart and their mother had declared herself "cooked" after Gunner came. The surprise of expecting at forty-two didn't start out delightful, but as soon as Lottie was born and the light emanating from her filled their family, everyone proclaimed her arrival as the greatest blessing ever bestowed on them.

Lottie had been born with Down syndrome. Due to his mom's diligence with the best treatments and therapists, Lottie was extremely high-functioning. She was in mainstream school and could read, loving romance novels. She was well loved by everyone and had been voted Prom Princess at her high school this year. Slade felt indebted and grateful to those kids for doing that for her. He and his three brothers had escorted her, and it had been a fabulous night. Preston and Jex had spent most of the night signing autographs, but they hadn't minded. Those students had given their sister a gift they couldn't repay.

Lottie was absolutely beautiful with her long, dark hair, rounded cheeks, and an ever-present sparkle in her deep brown eyes. His mom kept her dressed perfectly at all times. Slade was certain Lottie's outfits cost more than his business suits. Slade loved being around her, especially when he had the chance to help her with her charity.

"Hi, biggest bro," she said. "What's up?"

"I'm in a pretty town called Sausalito." He panned the video around to show her the quaint street, the ships lit up out in the bay, and the Golden Gate Bridge.

"Ooh, I want to go."

"Okay. I'll bring you back here." Maybe then he could finally have a date with Mae, or find Josie again. What would the two women think of Lottie? In high school it used to be his and his brothers' test to their dates. If the girls weren't nice to Lottie, the brothers didn't ask them out again, saying quietly to each other, "Well, now you know."

"You look fancy." She giggled. "Did you kiss a girl?"

Slade chuckled. He would think his sister was the most insightful person in the world if she didn't ask him that question regularly. "I did," he admitted, afraid he might regret saying so. Lottie would go nuts.

Lottie squealed, clapped her hands, then brought them both to her forehead and waved them, her gesture that she was really excited. "Was she pretty? Where is she? I want to say hi."

"I ... had to say goodbye to her." He tried to hide his despair. Josie seemed magical to him, even more so now that he'd lost her by his own choice. "But she was the most beautiful woman I've ever seen. Lit up from the inside, like you."

"Was she beautiful as me?"

"No one is as beautiful as you, my sister." The brothers loved that they could shower Lottie with words, love, and presents without ever spoiling her. She was angelic.

She giggled. "When do I meet her?"

Oh, man. How did he explain this to Lottie? "Um, it's like ..." He couldn't think of what chick flick it was like. "One of your movies when a man falls for a woman and kisses her, but he loses her and doesn't know her name to find her again." He didn't even dare get into the mess with Mae and his feelings for her. Lottie would flip.

Her eyes widened. "Oh, no! You lost her? So it's like *Sleepless in Seattle*."

His car pulled up and the driver rushed around to get his door. "Thanks," Slade mouthed, slipping inside. "How's it like *Sleepless in Seattle?"* Thank heavens for Lottie. She was helping ease his pain.

"They love each other, but they don't know each other."

Slade laughed. What he felt for Josie wasn't love. Yes, he was drawn to her and the kiss had been unreal, but he was also drawn to Mae. What would it be like to kiss Mae? Sadly, he couldn't even picture Mae's face, just those obnoxious glasses, but he could remember many of her funny quips and the way she made him feel—happy and not weighed down by the burdens of a billion-dollar business.

"So, you'll find her. It's fate." Lottie clapped her hands together again. "Yay!"

Slade felt a rock settle in his stomach. Easy to say in a chick flick or in an innocent girl's mind that he could find Josie again, but not so easy to do. He didn't even know if she was from Sausalito, and he lived across the country. He was flying out tonight, his plane on standby for after his date. He would be back home and back to work and his predictable life tomorrow. Most of the joy in his life came from Lottie and his brief conversations with Mae.

He changed the subject to what Lottie had been doing and got a full report of driving out to the Cape and playing in the freezing water with Gunner, who was on leave from the SEALs for a few weeks. Slade tried to focus on the conversation, but the feel of Josie in his arms crowded out almost everything else.

Mae slipped out of her beautiful dress and into some sweats and a T-shirt that said, "Bookmarks are for quitters." She pulled her hair into a ponytail, wiped off a lot of the makeup with a face-cleansing wipe, but didn't take the contacts out. With the fake eyelashes and the contacts, she thought she looked pretty, even without all the makeup, hair, and the gorgeous dress. Did she dare let Slade see her like this on their next video chat? Would he recognize she was Josie?

The doorbell rang, and she hurried for it. It rang over and over again before she yanked open the door. "The doorbell works," she said to Kit.

Kit rushed inside and flung her arms around her. "What happened? Are you okay?"

Mae leaned into her friend's hug. Kit and Kit's mom were the only physical touch Mae ever experienced, except for Slade's. She pulled back and snapped her fingers. "That's it!"

"What's it?"

"The unreal connection, the sparks, the overwhelming desire, and all that junk. It was inflated because I can't remember the last time a man really touched me. Right?" Kit's brothers and dad were very good men, but they didn't grab Mae and hug her. Usually a handshake or a pat on the arm was their greeting or goodbye.

Kit shook her head. "I don't think so. Wait! You felt connection, sparks, and *overwhelming* desire when he touched you?"

"Kit, he kissed me," she had to admit.

Kit screamed and hugged her again. "And it was good?"

"Fabulous. Like better than anything I've read in a book."

"Welcome to the big leagues." Grinning, Kit tugged her toward the couch and pulled her down. "Tell me all."

Mae relayed the story, word for word. Kit grimaced and cheered at appropriate times. When she finished, Mae said, "So?"

"You messed it all up," Kit confirmed. "But then he kind of did too, at least at the end. He didn't recognize you, and then he let the waiter manipulate the situation. Most importantly, why did he send Josie away after that fabulous kissing session?" She stood and started pacing the room. Mae watched her, letting her work it out. "You know, there are a lot of positives, though."

"Yeah, I can live vicariously through my own memories until I'm old, fat, and gray."

"Baloney! You aren't living through any memories; you're going to make more. You love Slade Steele?"

Mae nodded. There was no reason to deny it to her best friend.

Kit smiled. "You had an amazing connection with him?"

"As Josie." Truly she felt a connection to him every day through video chats as herself, but that probably meant nothing to Slade.

"Doesn't matter. He felt it, and you did too. And boys aren't like us; they don't hold silly grudges for a woman not telling them the truth."

"O-kay."

"Slade's the one I feel bad for. We have all the cards. He doesn't know that Josie's you. He doesn't even know Josie's last name."

"So, what do we do?"

"He's got to be miserable right now, going insane. He shared this unreal moment with Josie then told her that he wants Mae."

"Sort of." He had said he thought Mae was amazing and said her name all beautifully after they kissed, so there was that.

"Don't you discount yourself. You're the best, and obviously Slade has seen that, even through the frumpy clothes and huge glasses." Kit nodded. "We're going to let him stew for a few weeks then we're going to do something insane." Her blue eyes lit up.

"What?" Mae didn't like the sound of this. Kit's insane ideas in high school had always gotten the two of them in trouble, once even with the law.

"We're going to fly to Boston, and you are going to march into his office dressed like Josie, kiss the dickens out of him, and tell him you're really Mae. I can just envision it, and I love it!"

Mae stood to face her friend and shook her head. "No way. Even if I was brave enough to do that, I can't drive across a *bridge*." She flung her hand in the Golden Gate Bridge's direction. "How am I going to fly across the country?"

Kit looked compassionately at her. "That's why we're going to let him stew for a few weeks. He'll be fit to be tied wanting both you and Josie, and Mom and I will be praying nonstop to give you strength to overcome your fears."

Mae's stomach tightened. She loved her friend, and though it was terrifying, she also loved the idea of marching into Slade's office, kissing him, and telling him the truth. Yet how could she overcome her fears in this life?

Kit squeezed her hands. "Will you pray with me?"

Mae's throat was dry, but she nodded. They bowed their heads, and Mae silently but fervently added her pleas to Kit's. It would take a miracle equivalent to walking on water to get her across that devil bridge and on an airplane.

CHAPTER EIGHT

Mae slept through workouts in the morning, ignoring Kit's texts and phone calls. The prayer and support from her friend had helped last night, but by midnight she'd succumbed to depression over the way things had ended with Slade, and the certainty she'd never feel his mouth on hers again. She'd consumed a container of Ben & Jerry's strawberry cheesecake ice cream, then couldn't sleep because of her bellyache and her heartache.

She rolled out of bed and jammed her glasses on. Kit had made her promise that she'd get back to the eye doctor and buy a large box of contacts. She would. Tomorrow. Today she was going to stay in her glasses and her frumpy T-shirt. She wouldn't deal with anything more strenuous than work issues she couldn't ignore. She'd go outside and savor her beautiful spot of earth—go on some walks down to the water, or maybe take a bike ride up to Mill Valley and the waterfall.

The unique ring from her video chats with Slade sounded, and her stomach flipped. He was calling her. What should she say? Would it be awkward? What if he figured everything out? *Please let him figure everything out*, she begged the good Lord. That would be so much easier than her conquering her fears.

She ran to her computer, pushing the answer button before she could second-guess herself. "Hi!" she said brightly.

"Hi, Mae." His voice wasn't cold, but it definitely wasn't his normal warm, friendly, inspiring tones. His eyes swept over her. "Late night?"

Now the censure in his voice ripped through her. She'd also realized late last night that she'd never even responded to his last text pleading to still meet her even though she'd claimed to have left. He probably thought she was such a brat. Did he think she'd gone with some other man? How could she correct him without really correcting him? She and Kit had their plan to let him stew and dream about Josie while hopefully falling more for Mae through their video chats before she worked up her courage to get on that plane, but that all seemed pretty stupid right now. She wanted to just spill the truth, then beg him to fly back to her.

"Um ... yeah." She tried to straighten her ponytail and then her shirt. She probably looked horrific, but Slade had never cared that she wasn't fixed up. He'd told Josie that he was interested in Mae. Last night already felt like a fairy tale that she hadn't really been a part of, except for her body, which still tingled at the memory of his touch and him staring at her like she was the most beautiful woman in the world. If only he'd look at her like that right now ... but he was looking at her as if she had ditched him and then gone with another man. Cripes!

He nodded, a muscle working in his jaw and his lips tight. "So, on the Keller file." He proceeded to move straight into business.

Mae tried to remember Kit's instructions to be her funny self, but hardly any original quips came to her, and when they did, he barely cracked a smile. Her stomach was tied in pretzels by the time they got through the projects she needed to work on.

"I like your shirt," he muttered, and Mae took the slightly personal sentence as the first good sign of this phone call.

She glanced down. Her shirt read, "If you don't like tacos, I'm nacho type." "Thanks," she murmured. Swallowing hard, she tried to be brave and said, "Do *you* like tacos?"

The first real smile she'd seen from him today flitted across his face. "Yeah, I do." The smile disappeared, and he said, "Talk to you soon." She saw his finger stretching toward the screen to end the call.

"Hey," Mae said quickly before she lost her nerve. "I'm ... sorry about last night."

His hand fell to his side and he studied her as if trying to peer past her glasses. "Me too." There was an awkward pause, and then he said, "I really wanted to meet you."

You did? Do you still? What about Josie? She wanted to grill him with questions. Instead she bit at her lip and then said, "Maybe we could try again. Go for tacos this time." The words were out before she could call them back. He probably didn't want to try again, and she didn't know if she dared try again. Last night had been tough and crazy and also magical. Those fabulous, insanely beautiful kisses were never far from her thoughts, but he hadn't kissed her as Mae.

He gave her a soft smile and said, "Maybe. Talk to you later." Then he was gone.

Mae sat staring at the screen, feeling like she'd lost him all over again.

Slade stared at the background of a waterfall on his computer screen. Mae was gone, and he felt lost without her. Last night was a missed opportunity with Mae, and it still stung that she'd left and then never responded to his text, but Mae was obviously socially backward and more than likely not his type. Yet he liked her, a lot. He also was attracted to and intrigued by Josie, and he wished he hadn't said Mae's name after they'd kissed, then put her in that taxi without getting her phone number or at the very least her last name.

He shook his head and focused on his computer, pulling up his email. Work was good. Work could distract him from the confusion of two women on his brain. It was crazy how drawn he was to Mae when he had never met her in person and couldn't really tell what she looked like behind those too-large glasses, but he was also incredibly drawn to Josie, whom he hardly knew. He kept telling himself the draw to Josie was all physical and shallow, but some part of him didn't believe it. Josie had been so much more than a pretty package.

Trying to shut it from his mind, he got to work.

A week passed, and the memory of Josie somewhat faded, but he never lost the feeling of connection, desire, and—did he dare even think it?—love that he'd experienced when he'd touched and kissed her. If he believed Lottie's chick flicks, he'd think he lost his chance with his soul mate.

He was getting comfortable with Mae again, laughing at her jokes, and looking forward to any chance he had to video chat her. She'd also started texting him, sending him pictures of funny memes or T-shirts, or simply chatting about their day. He was afraid to suggest he fly out to meet her again. What if it all spiraled downward? What if he ran into Josie and got even more confused? He felt like he was falling for Mae and like he'd already fallen for Josie. Josie was out of his reach and he needed to forget her. Did he dare suggest Mae fly here? He could call it a work trip for her to meet people in his Boston offices that she associated with through video chat, email, and text.

Yet he still couldn't forget Josie. He realized late Saturday night, when he was home alone, that he wanted to find her, give her a chance. She'd been delightful to talk with, even before he touched her; maybe they could have as much fun chatting as he and Mae did. He wasn't sure what was pushing him to find Josie. It may have been due to the fact that he hadn't talked to Mae since yesterday during work hours, or it may have been that Lottie had forced him to watch *Sleepless in Seattle* and then grilled him, "Did it feel like that, like magic, when you touched Josie's hand?"

He'd had to admit that it had felt even more powerful than Meg Ryan and Tom Hanks had portrayed. He was a mess.

Finding the number for Sushi Sticks, he dialed it and asked after the greetings, "Can I please talk to Dirk Miller? I believe he's a waiter there."

The lady paused. "Um, he's not here right now, but I can ask him to call you."

Slade thanked her and gave her his name and number before ending the call. His penthouse overlooked the open area of Boston Commons. He stared out his floor-to-ceiling windows at the softly lit park below, his phone in hand. He was tempted to call Mae. Chatting with her late at night like this would be a soothing balm and might push them completely out of the employer/employee relationship. He wanted that, but if he found Josie and fell for her, he didn't want to lead Mae on.

His phone rang, and he startled. The number was unknown, but the area code was the same as Mae's, so he assumed it could be Dirk. "Hello?"

"Slade." A confident voice came through the line. "Dirk Miller. You needed something?"

This man was not who he pretended to be, but that wasn't Slade's problem. "You were my waiter a week ago."

"Yes, sir." The "sir" was said with a twinge of sarcasm. "How did it go with ... Josie, was it?"

Slade didn't think this guy deserved an explanation, but he needed his help. "Great, until I kissed her and then said another woman's name."

"Whoa. Nice one."

"Yeah, not really." He thought of how much razzing his suave brother, Jex, would have given him if he'd been there. As he paced his living area, his feet tapped loudly on the distressed wood floor. "I obviously messed it up, and then, because I felt awkward for calling her the wrong name, I immediately flagged a taxi for her, apologized, and let her leave. I don't even know her name or if she lives in the Bay Area. Do you know her? Have you seen her again?"

"Sorry, man." Dirk's tone was considerably softer. "I haven't seen her again, and I'd never seen her before that night. She was an impressive lady, though, wasn't she?"

"Yes, she was." Slade's hopes deflated. "If you ever see her, would you tell her ... I'm sorry and I'd love to see her again?"

"Sure. Sorry I can't help more."

"No worries. You have my number. Take care."

"You too."

Slade hung up the phone and wished he would've stayed at his parents' place in Duxbury. Going to church with them, Lottie, and Gunner in the morning and having Sunday brunch sounded much better than being alone. Maybe alone was what he was destined for. It wasn't as if he could declare his love to either Mae or Josie when he didn't know which woman he truly wanted to pursue. The fact that he wanted to date both of them didn't make him very proud of himself.

His phone beeped an incoming text. He grinned when he read the message from Mae with a picture of a T-shirt.

Just found this online. Buy it? "I'm a secondhand vegetarian. Cows eat grass. I eat cows."

He texted back. *Definitely buy it.*

It's funny?

Almost as funny as you. I love your sense of humor. And he did. He loved so many things about Mae. If only he could be assured that when he touched her there would be even a tenth of the spark and desire he'd felt with Josie. He paused and then typed quickly before he could veto himself. *I can't wait to see you in it.*

She sent back a smiley face. *Thanks. We'll taco 'bout you seeing me soon.*

I'm game for tacos or talking anytime. He truly meant it.

Night. Happy Sabbath tomorrow.

Good night.

His phone stopped beeping and he felt the letdown of saying goodbye to Mae. The whole sparks thing was pretty overrated. He'd rather be with someone he could talk and laugh with—but if that was true, why could he still feel Josie in his arms?

CHAPTER NINE

"Please, please, please come eat sushi with me." As Kit tugged Mae toward the restaurant, she pouted her lower lip—an expression that probably worked wonders on any male of the species. Sushi Sticks was the restaurant of doom in her mind.

"Come on, Kit. Let's go for a greasy hamburger dripping with barbecue sauce." Mae tried to say it all tantalizing with an appealing wink, but that just wasn't her style. She was dressed nice for her today in a stretchy gray skirt, paired with one of her favorite T-shirts that Kit had tied in a knot at her waist to give it some shape. Her hair was down and her contacts were in. She even put on a little of the lip stain Kit had left for her, and though she'd never admit it to Kit, she didn't even notice wearing the lip stain. The fake eyelashes were nice because she didn't need any other eye makeup with them on.

"I'm craving sushi, and I think it'll be good to relive your night as we consume it. I'll get yours deep-fried if you're wanting something greasy."

Mae scowled at her. She loved her sushi deep-fried, and Kit never failed to tease her about it. She didn't want to relive that night, except for teasing with and kissing Slade as Josie, but she let Kit pull her through the doors. Instead of feeling the panic she'd expected, she remembered seeing Slade's handsome face for the first time in person. She adored him and there was no way to deny it.

The hostess directed them to a table, thankfully not the one she'd been at that night. They settled in and ordered three rolls more than they could ever finish, and then Kit grabbed Mae's hand. "Okay, sweet friend. It's been almost two weeks, and I have been praying my guts out. I'm so in tune with heaven currently that I may just get translated and you'll have to say goodbye to your best friend." She winked. "Please tell me all my efforts aren't in vain. Are you ready to fly to Boston?"

Mae worried her lip. She'd been praying also, but she hadn't received any confirmation that she could handle driving across the bridge, load into an airplane, and fly across the nation. Slade was amazing, but she'd decided to alter the prayer request Kit had given her, asking instead that he'd come back to Sausalito to see her.

"Come on. I'll be right by your side. I ordered you several of your funny T-shirts, but fitted, and I figure the first one that shows up will be the lucky shirt that gets to be touched by Slade and our sign that we need to catch a plane. I know exactly what I'll have you wear with the T-shirt and how I'll do your hair.

Slade is gonna flip when you strut into his office as Josie-slash-Mae. Can I watch?"

Mae's stomach churned. She might not be able to eat any of the seven rolls they'd ordered. Forget the terror of flying. What about the terror of strutting into Slade's office? They'd gotten comfortable again, teasing and laughing on video calls, phone calls, and through texts. Last Saturday, she'd texted the *second-hand vegetarian* quote. He'd told her he loved her sense of humor and couldn't wait to see her in the T-shirt. Then he'd taken it to the next level and said he was game for tacos anytime. She probably should've asked him right then to meet up, but she'd chickened out. She'd still gone to bed with a huge grin on her face, thinking through their conversations. Slade was amazing, but she didn't know if she could overcome all her fears to tell him the truth, kiss him, then tell him how much she loved him. Couldn't he just fly here and they try out the kissing part again?

"Hey," a deep male voice said from above them. "You're back."

Mae glanced up and saw that the handsome waiter with the bright blue eyes from the other night was grinning at her.

His gaze slipped to Kit, and his grin got even more appealing. "Is this the friend?"

Mae laughed. She'd forgotten she'd told him she'd set him up with her gorgeous friend. "Yes, sir."

"What do you mean, 'the friend'?" Kit's eyes narrowed suspiciously, but Mae could see the glint in their blue depths. She was interested. Definitely.

"I'll explain later," Mae said.

"I'll take the setup anytime," the waiter said.

"Who are you and why should I care?" Kit asked, giving him a flirtatious flutter of her eyelashes and making the smart-alecky words sound like a sassy come-on. Dang, she was good. Mae had a feeling this guy may be just as practiced in the art of flirting. Might be a good challenge for Kit. Every man fell for her upon first sight.

"He's the waiter who ... helped me," Mae explained.

"Dirk," the guy offered, smiling at Kit. He turned to Mae and chuckled. "I like your shirt."

Mae glanced down, unsure what she'd thrown on today. She'd been making an effort to wear her contacts, put on minimal makeup, and brush out her hair after Slade and she had their video chat done for the day, but she still wasn't dolled to the nines like Kit. Her shirt read, *"That's too much bacon," said no one. Ever.*

"Words to live by," Mae said.

Dirk laughed again, then dropped a bomb in her lap. "Slade Steele called me."

Mae leaned back. "What? I didn't know you knew him." Had he and Slade set her up that night?

"I don't. He tracked me down, asking about ... Josie. He asked me, if I saw you, to tell you sorry and he'd love to see you again. I didn't feel right telling him any more information about you, but when you walked in, I wanted to at least relay the message." His smile slid quickly back to Kit. "And take you up on your offer."

"Sorry? He said he was sorry?" Sorry that he sent her away that night? Sorry that he kissed her? Sorry that he called her Mae after he kissed Josie?

He'd tried to track her down and told Dirk that he wanted to see her again. That was incredible news and truly all that mattered. The poor guy didn't know how she was playing him, and she didn't want to be playing him, but it was too scary to get on that plane to Boston. She'd teased and tried to get him to come here again, but he hadn't taken the bait yet. Maybe she should just tell him in a video chat who she was, but it didn't suit. She wanted to tell him in person, apologize, and then kiss and kiss and kiss until she ran out of oxygen and passed out in his arms.

"He really seemed desperate to find you again." Dirk shrugged. "Sorry, that's all I know. That, and I do have his number on my call list if you want it."

"I know it already."

He smiled at that. "I thought you might. Good luck." He nodded to her then turned to Kit. "I'll see *you* around." He winked, handed a business card to Kit, and then he was gone.

Kit fanned herself with the card. "Sheesh. You do attract the hot, confident men." She glanced at the card. "Dirk Miller." She turned it over. "Weird. No title. Only a phone number. Does that mean I should call him? He was your waiter?"

Mae nodded, distracted. Not that she didn't care about Kit's love life, but Kit went through several men a day. Falling in love and settling down was such a future concept to Kit, discussing it would be fruitless. The hot waiter would mean nothing to her, and Slade meant everything to Mae.

"What do I do?" Mae asked.

"Well, it sounds like Slade is still interested in Josie, but he's been super cute with you as Mae, right?"

"Last night he said he loved my sense of humor and couldn't wait to see my T-shirt in person."

"Okay. I think we've confused the poor man enough. It's time to take action." Kit took a deep breath. "The day the first T-shirt arrives, we catch the next plane to Boston. Agreed?"

"I'm so scared, Kit."

"Of what?"

"Of everything!"

"I'll be there. The Lord will be there. Between the two of us, we can help you secure your destiny."

Mae reached for her friend's hand. "Can we pray right now?"

"For sure. And don't worry. I've got lots of ideas of how to keep you calm."

"Good, because I've got none."

CHAPTER TEN

Mae straightened her ponytail and her T-shirt, pushed her glasses into place, and answered the call from Slade. "Hey, you, how goes the morning?"

"Better now." He gave her his full smile, and Mae barely stopped herself from sighing and putting a hand to her heart. "How about you?" he asked.

"Well, to start, Kit made me do fifty burpees, a hundred split jumps, a hundred air squats, a hundred bridge walkouts, fifty tuck jumps, and gym slides until I cried uncle at five a.m., so I can hardly sit in this chair."

"And all I did was run along the piers and through Boston Commons."

"You've got a cush life, my friend." How she wished they were more than friends. Maybe today would be the day her T-shirt would arrive and she and Kit would hop a plane to Boston.

Nerves assaulted her at the very thought.

Slade let out a bark of a laugh. "Yeah, owning and managing over a dozen loan offices is easy stuff."

"Easy peasy lemon squeezy. Good thing you have me."

His smile softened. "Good thing." He squinted and read her shirt. "'I kiss better than I cook'?" His voice went low and husky. "Is that true?"

Mae shrugged, biting at her lip and wishing she knew how to flirt. The mere tone of his voice gave her heart palpitations and sweaty palms. "For sure. But that might only be because I'm a horrific cook, so I'm not sure the kissing would be up to your high expectations." She gasped after she said it.

Slade's eyes widened; then he chuckled. "Maybe we'll see when we meet up for tacos."

"M-maybe." Oh my goodness, did that mean he wanted to kiss her? As Mae! That was the way she was interpreting it. She wanted to scream and dance and find Kit and scream and dance some more. She really wanted to kiss him, but that would require flying to Boston. *Please help me be strong, Lord*, she repeated over and over again in her mind.

"Mae? Mae?"

"Oh, sorry, got distracted." She gave him a bold wink, even though he probably couldn't see it through her glasses. She was very impressed with herself at the moment, and even more impressed with Slade. He wanted to meet for tacos and maybe kiss her. Yeah, baby!

"I can see that." He chuckled again and then said, "The Phoenix office is misinterpreting some of the guidelines on the FHA changes. Can you do a chat with them today, and have them go through all the FHA loans they've closed since the changes took effect to catch any errors?"

"Yes, sir." The business end of the conversation continued, and before she knew it, they were saying goodbye.

"So, about those tacos?" Slade said before he hung up, staring intently at her as if he could peer past her glasses.

Mae was so happy right now. "Yeah, about those tacos ..."

"Are you coming to me, or am I flying out there?"

Mae blinked at him, praying she wouldn't pass out from happiness. He'd come to her, even after he thought she'd stood him up last time. She loved him even more. It would be better to have him come here. She wouldn't have to conquer any fears.

"How soon could you come?" she asked, her voice quivering.

"Let me look." He paused and searched through his phone, his brow furrowed. "It'd be late next week before I could get away for a few days."

A few days? He wanted to spend a few days with frumpy Mae and her big glasses? What reality was she living in? She was deliriously happy right now. How would he react to her in contacts and with her hair down? Yet he might be upset that she'd pretended to be Josie and had been too big of a wimp to tell him the truth.

"Do we ... need a few days for tacos?" she asked.

Slade looked her over and nodded. "I think a few days might be a good start to our taco time." He smiled. "I really want to get to know you better, Mae."

She did squeal then, and it made him laugh. "What if I came to you?" She clapped her hand over her mouth. She couldn't believe she'd just said that. He was willing to come to her, but not until next week. She didn't want to wait until next week. She'd put this off long enough. What if he changed his mind before then, found someone else, or decided he wanted Josie instead of her?

Slade's eyebrows rose, and he said, "I'd love that. How soon could you come?"

"You're my boss. You say."

"I'm sending my plane in the next few minutes. It takes five hours to fly there. I'll text you the coordinates to the private airport in San Francisco. A driver will be waiting to bring you straight to my apartment."

Mae's head spun with his decisive words. It was so appealing how he'd phrased that. She tilted and almost fell off her chair.

"Mae?" he asked when she didn't respond. "You okay? I can get you a hotel room as well."

She swallowed hard and squeaked out of her very dry throat. "Okay. Definitely okay. I can get my own hotel room."

His brow furrowed as if he wanted to plan every detail of her trip, but he only said, "I'll see you tonight, then?"

"Yes, sir, you will."

"I can't wait." He grinned at her, and she grinned back. The moment was beautiful, and she wanted to freeze-frame it for the rest of her life. The anticipation to see him again, touch him, and kiss him almost overwhelmed her. "See you soon," he said huskily, and then he was gone.

Mae fell off her chair then. She landed on the floor and squealed and giggled, and then she rolled onto her knees and prayed. Her dreams were coming true, but she still had to get across the Golden Gate Bridge and onto an airplane. Slade's airplane. Her wealthy, handsome, charming boss, who might actually want to date her. Whew, it was getting thick and scary. Hopefully Kit truly had some tricks up her sleeve.

———

Slade hung up with Mae and smiled. Bringing Mae here felt right. He was interested in her and wanted to get to know her. Mae was so great, and if there were no sparks and it didn't work between them, he felt like she'd understand and keep being friends and working for him. He hoped so, at least. He'd hate to lose her as an employee or a friend, but he'd hate even more to never take this chance.

Josie was still in the back of his mind, but she was a dream, a fairy tale, a chick flick that was never going to come true. Lottie wouldn't be happy with him for giving up that fantasy, as she often brought Josie up and asked when he was going to miraculously find her again. Lottie had even told their military brother, Gunner, the story and begged him to find a private investigator to track down Josie. Slade had been tempted but told Gunner to hold off. If things with Mae didn't pan out, he'd try that route. Josie felt like a fictitious character at this point, but Mae was real, and he loved every interaction with her. Why not take a chance?

His visions of taking off Mae's glasses, tugging her hair out of that ponytail, and seeing if she did kiss better than she cooked were going to come true tonight. He glanced at his watch. It was nine a.m. Best-case scenario, she'd be with him by seven. He'd try to focus on work for a few hours, and then he was going to get his apartment and himself ready. He'd have a catered dinner ready, flowers, romantic music, waiting in a suit, the whole deal. Might as well go all in and see what panned out.

As he focused back on his computer, he was grinning to himself.

CHAPTER ELEVEN

Mae called Kit and simply demanded, "Get here now. We're flying to Boston this afternoon."

"No way! Yes!" Kit hung up, and two excruciating hours later, she was banging on Mae's front door. She had two suitcases and some clothes and shoes in hand. She hugged Mae and said, "Sorry it took so long. I had to finish work and get everything ready. What happened? Tell me all!"

"Slade invited me to come for ... tacos and kissing." Mae flipped her ponytail and pretended a confidence she didn't feel. "He's sending his plane!"

Kit swayed on the porch, and then she jumped in the air like a cheerleader and started screaming. They hugged and laughed, and Kit made her recite everything Slade had said. Then Kit pushed Mae into the house and handed her a T-shirt. "This is so fate. I ordered several different funny T-shirts that will actually be your size and flatter you, and look which one showed up today. It's your taco saying!"

Mae looked at the dusty rose T-shirt that read, "If you don't like tacos, I'm nacho type." She thought the good Lord must be answering Kit's nonstop prayers. Maybe her parents and sisters were up in heaven orchestrating this day. She didn't know how things worked on the other side, but indescribable peace and warmth settled over her. Tears pricked at the corners of her eyes, then spilled over.

"Don't cry," Kit exclaimed. "You don't have to wear it. I thought he said something about tacos."

"It's perfect, Kit. It's absolutely perfect. I'm crying because I'm so happy. I feel like my parents and sisters have a hand in this too."

"Ah, sweetie." Kit hugged her tightly. "I'm sure they do. You deserve every happiness." She pulled back and smiled, and her eyes got a cunning look in them. "Okay, my turn to have fun!"

Kit burned the remaining time by fixing Mae up. Mae protested that she needed to get some real work done, but Kit said she'd let her work on the plane.

She kept making Mae rehearse exactly what Slade had said; then she'd squeal and repeat, "He honestly said he was sending his plane in a few minutes, all decisive, sexy, and alpha male?" Kit clapped her hands together and grinned. "I'm so in love with him."

"It was very sexy," Mae agreed, reliving it in her mind. "And I'm the one in love with him. Remembering the whole conversation just gives me the butterflies. Do you really think he wants to kiss Mae?" She wrinkled her nose and looked herself over in the mirror. From top to bottom, she was perfect and mostly Josie—fitted black skirt, high-heeled teal canvas shoes, hair and makeup expertly done—but the T-shirt was all Mae. Slade would be waiting for her at his apartment, so he'd know it was Mae coming in, but what if he got mad that she'd tricked him?

"I think he does. He's a great guy, Mae, and he's obviously not only concerned about looks. He's fallen for you with glasses covering your eyes and half your face, no makeup, and your hair not done. That's really cool and really rare. I'm not trying to say most of the world is shallow, but ..." Kit shrugged. "We are, but you're not. You're genuine. Please don't second-guess this. You're going to strut in there, and he's going to pass out. Then you can resuscitate him with your kiss." She giggled.

A honk sounded from outside, so Mae didn't have time to respond to all of her friend's sweet words.

"There's our Uber. Let's go!"

The expected nerves washed over her, and she grabbed Kit's hand. "I'm scared, Kit."

"Of what?"

"Of everything."

Kit nodded. "I know, sweetie. I'll be right there. Oh, I almost forgot! I talked to Dr. Gray a few days ago, and he called in a prescription for you for Valium. Will you take it? He says one should be enough to help you be relaxed on the bridge and the plane. I was supposed to give it to you an hour ago, but I forgot."

Mae's stomach was rolling. She didn't want to take a prescription drug, but she really needed some kind of help, or she was going to be an absolute mess before she even got to Slade. She trusted Dr. Gray and Kit. They both knew her and her issues well. Maybe the Valium was help from above too and would sustain her through the next five hours. She nodded uncertainly.

Kit placed two small blue pills in her hand and handed her a bottle of water as the Uber driver honked again. She hurried off to open the front door and wave to let him know they were coming. Mae slipped one pill into a small pocket of her purse, threw the other pill in her mouth without letting herself second-guess it, and then chugged some water. Taking a deep breath, she clutched her purse and her carry-on suitcase. All kinds of cute clothes, dresses, and shoes were packed inside from Kit and Kit's mom for Mae to spend the next few days with Slade. She grinned. She was doing this, and it was going to be awesome.

They loaded into the Camry, the driver helping them with their suitcases. He was a nice guy, about their age. He immediately started hitting on Mae, making a quip about her T-shirt and how he liked tacos. She tried to be nice, but he had no clue what he was competing with. Ah, Slade.

When she gave one-word answers, the driver turned his attention to Kit. Mae looked out the window, her stomach getting tighter and tighter as they went up the hill, leaving Sausalito behind and approaching the Golden Gate Bridge. Nausea rose up her throat, and she started sweating. The driver was oblivious as he flirted with Kit.

"Stop! Pull over!" Mae screamed before he could enter the highway that led to the bridge.

The man yanked the car to the side of the road and glared back at her. "What's wrong?"

"Mae?" Kit's voice was full of understanding and concern. "You've got this."

Mae didn't have this. What was she doing? She stared at the orange towers of the bridge. She hated that bridge and all it had taken from her. Could she truly just sit here as they motored across? Pulling the second Valium pill out of her purse, she shoved it in and swallowed it dry.

"Mae?" Kit sounded so apprehensive.

"I can't do this," she muttered. Slade had said he'd come to her. Next week wasn't that long to wait.

"You can. Do it for Slade, but also do it for you. You're stronger than some stupid bridge."

Mae focused on her friend.

Kit nodded encouragingly. "I believe in you."

Mae swallowed hard and pushed out a breath.

"Can we go now?" the driver asked impatiently.

"Mae?"

Mae said a prayer and squeezed her eyes shut. "Let's go."

That was all the encouragement the driver needed as he darted onto the road that led to the bridge.

Kit squeezed her hand and murmured, "You're doing great."

"Those pills aren't working." Mae clung to Kit's hand. "I'm going to puke."

The driver glanced sharply back at her. "What?"

"Look at the road!" Mae yelled.

He whipped back around but said, "Don't puke in my car. I can't pull over on the bridge."

"She's fine," Kit insisted. "Please unlock our windows." The guy complied, and Kit rolled both rear windows down, gingerly leaning over Mae to reach hers. "Look out at the ocean. Take some deep breaths. You're going to be all right."

Mae tried to comply, but her deep breaths felt a lot more like hyperventilating. She obeyed Kit's instructions and watched the ocean, focusing on ignoring the bridge completely. A suffocating fear pressed down on her, though, and her hands were so clammy she could hardly hold on to Kit.

This was where she'd lost her family. Her parents and sisters had been her everything. Besides Kit. Guilt swept over her afresh. She'd chosen to stay with Kit that fateful day and go on a bike ride to Mill Valley instead of supporting her sisters at their dance competition in San Francisco. How many times had she wished she'd gone to heaven with them? Yet if that was true, why was she so afraid of this bridge? She could die on it and be with them. That was a morbid thought. *Look at the ocean. Look at the ocean.* She felt cold and slimy all over. Horns beeped, and the sound of tires rumbling over the bridge and the smell of exhaust made her stomach churn even more.

Suddenly the final orange metal beams appeared, and then they were off the bridge.

"You did it!" Kit wrapped her arm around her and squeezed. "I'm so proud."

Mae blinked and looked around. She *had* done it. Glancing back at the bridge, a sense of awe overcame her. She'd done it! She'd come off the victor with her biggest fear. The bridge hadn't taken her down. She'd made it across—for Slade.

Next step was to fly across the country and then to walk into Slade's arms. She could do this. Her stomach settled, and she looked around at the city and the different green spaces they drove past. When they drove into the airport, the Uber driver had to give Mae's name to get clearance. They pulled up to a sleek white jet with a pilot and a stewardess all crisply dressed and waiting for them with large smiles. She wondered about that alternate reality again.

"Can I really pull this off?" she asked Kit, doubts creeping back in. "I'm just Mae."

"You are the amazing and fabulous Mae Delaney, and you are going to rock Slade Steele's world."

"Thanks." But she knew the depths of Kit's loyalty. Of course she had to say that.

They climbed out of the Uber, and the stewardess and pilot were all things gracious as they shook their hands, took their luggage, and gestured for them to climb aboard the beautiful plane. The inside was tan leather and wood accents. It was luscious.

"I guess if you've gotta fly ..." Kit quipped.

"Right?" Mae laughed, but that queasiness was back in her stomach. This was Slade's plane. The man had his own plane. Saying he was out of Mae's league didn't even come close to describing the discrepancy between them.

They got settled in, and the pilot informed them they'd take off in the next few minutes. The stewardess got them both a bottled water, and they assured her they didn't need anything else. She made sure their seat belts were fastened, then disappeared into a back room.

"Wowzers," Kit muttered. "I am so jealous of you right now."

"Jealous? Of the fact that I'm going to puke all over Slade's beautiful airplane?"

"No more puke talk. You're going to meet your dream man. He sent this piece of luxury for you. You're going to marry Slade Steele and be a billionairess. Don't forget your best friend when that happens."

"Marry?" Mae said faintly. "Please stop. I don't want to throw up."

"Then don't. If you mess up your breath and lipstick with vomit, I will beat you."

"Are you even going to let me eat before I meet him?"

"I'll think about it."

Mae rolled her eyes and pulled her phone out of her purse. "I told Slade I'd text him when we took off." She sent a picture of the plane and a quick text, trying for confident and funny. *This rocks! Thank you for sending the Batplane. See you soon.*

He texted back. *It's my favorite jet. Can't wait.*

His favorite jet? She wanted to tease about it, but the idea that he had multiple jets was throwing her back into the thoughts of him being way out of her league. Slade Steele. Who was she to think she could secure Slade Steele's affection?

Crazily enough, her stomach was actually settling, and she was starting to feel relaxed and kind of sleepy. Exhaustion crept in sneakily, but she was in an almost euphoric state. Maybe it was the thought of seeing Slade's smile, touching him, possibly kissing him. Maybe it was taking two Valium pills. Had Dr. Gray only suggested one? Kit had handed her two. Who cared? She felt amazing.

She leaned her head back and grinned like a fool. "Marry Slade," she murmured.

She didn't remember much else past that. The plane lifted into the air and she whooped when it did. Her eyelids got unbearably heavy, and she must've fallen asleep. The next thing she knew was Kit shaking her shoulder and begging her to wake up.

Mae managed to climb to her feet. Leaning heavily on Kit, she stumbled out of the airplane, gushing thanks to the pilot and stewardess, and then they were in the back of a nice car—she had no clue what kind it was. The lights of the freeway were flying past them, and she was so tired. She closed her eyes again.

Seconds later, Kit was shaking her and muttering all manner of things—Slade couldn't meet her like this, the dosage must've been too high, and asking her over and over again where her phone was.

Mae had no clue why Slade couldn't meet her or where her phone was. She nodded off again, and then she was clinging to Kit and they were waddling through a hotel lobby. Somehow they made it to an elevator, and finally she was stretched out on a soft bed.

"Ah, so soft. So tired. Can I see Slade soon?"

"Oh, Mae, I messed this all up."

"No. You're the best friend anyone could ever have."

"Not so sure about that." Kit sighed. "We've got to get that shirt off of you."

Mae tried to help out as Kit worked her T-shirt and shoes off, then slid her into the covers. "I love you, Kit." She rolled over and blessedly fell asleep again.

———

Slade had everything ready by seven p.m., and then he had nothing to do but wander his apartment, glancing at the clock every other minute as the delicious aroma of steak, pork, and chicken tacos floated to him. He finally got a notice from the pilot at eight-fifteen that they'd landed. His stomach rumbled with hunger but also with anticipation. Mae was very different, understated compared to Josie's incredible beauty, but they shared the same internal light. He hoped he was doing the right thing tonight and not leading Mae on. If there weren't any sparks or connection when he touched her like he'd felt with Josie, he would have to be honest and explain to her about the magical moments he'd shared with Josie. Maybe hire that private investigator. *Please let there be at least embers with Mae*, he prayed. Josie was incredible, but nobody was as funny and appealing to him as Mae—on video chat and text, that is. Maybe in person they'd be awkward and have no lasting connection.

He paced the apartment some more, grateful the food was all on warmers and would be fine. What would it be like when he finally met Mae? Would she hug him, or be shy until they got comfortable? Nerves made his empty stomach even more upset. Minutes ticked slowly by, and he started worrying. She should've been here by now. He thought she'd text him when they landed like she had when they took off, but nothing.

He sent a picture of the food and said, *Tacos are ready because I am your type.* Pushing send, he waited and stewed and finally let himself eat a few chips to get something in his sick stomach.

His phone rang, and he jumped. Glancing at it, he saw it was his driver, John. "How's it going?" he greeted him with, fighting the disappointment it wasn't Mae.

"Well, sir, I don't know how to tell you this, but the girls I picked up from your airplane—"

"Girls?"

"Yes. A blonde and a brunette. Very beautiful, classy-looking ladies."

Did his driver pick up the wrong women? Why would Mae bring someone with her? Although Slade thought Mae was attractive, he doubted someone else would call her "very beautiful," and with the casual way she dressed, classy-looking didn't fit either.

"I brought them to your building, but the brunette was ... maybe drunk? I don't know. She couldn't stay awake and was slurring her words. The blonde was beside herself muttering about you and how she'd messed this all up, and finally she asked me to take them to their hotel."

"What hotel?"

"Taj Boston."

The Taj was close to his building, right on Boston Commons. It was a nice hotel. "Thanks for letting me know."

"Yes, sir." John hung up.

Slade glanced at his texts. No response from Mae. What was going on with her? When he'd gone to Sausalito, she'd ditched him and didn't respond. Was it happening again? He pushed the call button on her number and waited as it rang five times, then went to voicemail. His jaw clenched. He'd been so excited to meet her, and now she was ditching him again.

Rushing out of his penthouse apartment, he waited impatiently for the elevator, hardly able to force a smile at the flirtatious lady who lived two floors below him. He waited for her to exit; the gentlemanly behavior had been drilled into him from his mother, or else he would've pushed ahead. Then he hurried out a side door, and as he started across the Commons, he ran.

He burst through the entrance to the Taj and beelined to the front desk. Thankfully, the lobby was empty besides him and the attendant.

The blonde grinned at him. "Hello, sir, may I help you?"

"Did Mae Delaney check in here? About half an hour ago?"

"Well, sir, I can't give out guest information."

"I know. I'm sorry." He shoved a hand through his hair. "Did you ever see *Sleepless in Seattle*?"

She looked taken aback, but then a soft smile lit her blue eyes. "Yeah, I did. When I was a little girl."

"My little sister claims it's like that. This woman means a lot to me, and we keep … missing each other." That wasn't completely true. Lottie had said that about Josie, not Mae, and he suspected Mae was ditching him, but he didn't know why. Confidence wasn't something he was short on, and he suspected it was more Mae dealing with some demons that he didn't understand, but he wanted to learn all about her and help her conquer them. "Can you please just tell me if she checked in?"

The lady hesitated, then tapped into her computer. Finally, she said, "I'm sorry, sir. Nobody under that name is registered."

Slade pushed out a frustrated breath. Why hadn't he forced the issue when she said she'd get her own hotel? Then he'd know exactly where she was. But he didn't want to be too pushy, and he couldn't have foreseen that she'd ditch him again. "Did two women come in about half an hour ago? A brunette and a blonde? The brunette maybe looked like she was drunk?"

The woman nodded slightly. "Yes."

Maybe someone who'd hijacked his plane was here. No, Mae had sent him that text from his plane. He was confused, tired, hungry, and frustrated. Had Mae just used him for a free flight on a private plane to Boston? Did she not care about him enough to even send him a text or call and say she couldn't make it tonight? Maybe she wasn't feeling well, maybe she was drunk. He didn't care; he just wanted to know what was going on. Why couldn't they ever match up?

He didn't think he should push this woman any more. "Thank you for the help," he murmured.

"Of course, sir."

Slade walked out of the Taj deflated and defeated. He pulled out his phone again but saw no return text and no return phone call. He stood outside in the muggy summer night and tried one more time. The call went to voicemail, but he said, "Mae. I don't know why you didn't come to me ... again. But I really want to meet you. Please call me back."

He hung up, feeling like the biggest sap on the planet. He was begging Mae to call him, and he didn't even know if they would go anywhere as a couple when they finally did meet. If there were no sparks or thrills when he touched Mae and he was forever caught up in how it felt to touch and kiss Josie, it wouldn't be fair to Mae to try to pursue a relationship simply because she was so funny and she grounded him.

He walked slowly across the Commons toward his building. His phone rang, and he almost dropped it in his excitement. An unknown number. Maybe it was Mae's friend. Maybe Mae had dropped her phone or something crazy like that.

"Hello," he rushed out.

"Sir. My name is Julie. I clean your plane."

Slade swallowed down the bitter disappointment. He was never going to find Mae. Maybe he could camp out in the lobby of Taj

Boston in the morning, but that wasn't his style. He was almost that desperate, though. Why wouldn't she come to him or call him?

"Yes, Julie," he said. "What can I do for you?"

"I found a phone on the floor, sir. It's got a floral case; I believe it's an iPhone. Would you like me to bring it to you?"

Could it be Mae's phone? Hope surged again. Maybe that was why she hadn't called him back. "Yes, please. I can drop you a pin with my location. Please bill me for the extra time." He'd give her a fat tip when she came as well.

"I'll be there soon, sir."

Slade hung up, relief washing over him. Maybe Mae hadn't completely ditched him. Maybe she'd gotten ... drunk on the plane? He didn't stock alcohol on his plane. At least there was a reason she wasn't responding to him if she didn't have her phone.

Now if only he could find her, get to the bottom of her issues, and kiss her until he knew if they should be together. Despite all the failed attempts, the lies he used to tell himself that he wasn't ready for a relationship, and who knew what fears or insecurities she was dealing with, he knew he wanted Mae.

CHAPTER TWELVE

Slade spent a restless night and skipped his morning workout. He didn't wait in the lobby of the Taj like he wanted to, but he waited outside on Boston Commons—pacing, watching, waiting. He couldn't unlock Mae's phone to call someone, but he prayed that maybe her friend would call it. He'd tried to do a video chat or send an email to her computer last night and gotten no response on either. He'd convinced himself that Mae had maybe taken something or gotten sick on the plane and that's why she hadn't come last night. It was the only way to keep himself from going insane.

As the early morning hours wore on and Mae didn't step through the doors of the Taj, his enthusiasm and hopes waned as well. Finally, he had no choice but to walk to his building, a few blocks away in the Financial District. He had a nine a.m. meeting he couldn't miss. If he knew for certain that Mae *hadn't* ditched him again, or used him for a girls' trip to Boston ... If he only knew she wanted him here waiting like some pathetic girl movie that Lottie would love, he would've missed any meeting. As it was, he had no clue where her intentions or thoughts were.

He called Lottie as he walked, needing a boost this morning.

"Hi, handsome bro," she called out. "How are you?"

"I'm not doing very well, Lottie. Mae ditched me."

"Who's Mae? You love Josie."

Slade pushed out a breath. "It's a mess, sis."

"Tell me all about it," she said, all mature and adorable.

Slade smiled, and as he walked, he proceeded to tell her the entire story. Lottie was uncharacteristically quiet when he finished. He was almost to his building and only had a few minutes to spare before his meeting, but he wanted to hear Lottie's thoughts.

"Why aren't you saying anything?" he asked.

"I'm trying to think what movie this is."

Slade chuckled. This was why he needed Lottie. It'd felt good to get it all off his chest, and only Lottie would be concerned about which of her chick movies his failed love life was like.

"Hmm. *Princess Diaries* or *Cinderella*," she declared.

Slade wasn't sure how she'd gotten there. "Why?"

"I think your Mae is ... dumpy? Is that right? But she's beautiful inside and she's going to transform into a princess."

Slade knew he hadn't used the word dumpy. That wasn't Mae at all, at least not to him. She was definitely beautiful on the inside, and he was attracted to the physical characteristics that he'd been able to glimpse through video chats—her mouth and her jawline, her smooth skin, and the obviously fit frame under her too-baggy T-shirts. He wasn't about to get into a discussion with Lottie about how Mae wasn't dumpy, though. "But why does she keep ditching the prince?" he asked instead.

A few men in business casual walking by looked at him strangely. Slade forced a smile.

"Because it's not easy to get to happy ever after. Come on, you know that, bro!"

Slade chuckled. "Okay. I'll give you that. So, what do I do?"

"Patience, my boy, patience," Lottie said solemnly. Slade's next youngest brother, Jex, the adventurer, was fond of that saying. Though Jex was crazy, he was also one of the most laid-back and patient people Slade knew.

Laughing, Slade managed to say, "I love you, Lottie."

"I love you too. When your princess finds you, bring her to see me. Please, please, please!"

"I will." Slade said goodbye and slid his phone in his pocket, rushing through the sliding glass doors and toward the elevator. If only his princess would find him.

CHAPTER THIRTEEN

Mae woke up with a pounding headache. Light streamed through the large windows, and she clapped a hand over her eyes. "Make the sun stop," she begged.

The room mercifully got darker. She blinked her eyes open again. "Tylenol?" she whimpered.

"I've got some." Kit rushed to her purse and returned a few seconds later with some pills, grabbing the complimentary water bottle off the counter.

Mae took the pills and washed them down with lukewarm water. "What happened?" she asked. She hated alcohol because her family had been killed by a drunk driver, so she'd never been hung over, but this must be what it felt like. "I can't remember much beyond you helping me off the plane, into a car, and then into the hotel."

"Oh, Mae, I'm so sorry. It had to be the Valium pills. I messed it all up."

Mae took a slow breath. "It's not your fault. I took them both."

"I gave you two of them?" Kit wrung her hands together.

"I took one initially and one in the car before the bridge. Where's my phone? Do you think I should text or call Slade, or should I try to get to him?" She groaned. "He's going to think I ditched him again."

"I don't know where your phone is. I wonder if you left it on the plane. I think you need to go to his office. The only way to fix this is in person. Let's get you showered and fixed up."

Mae nodded and struggled to her feet. Her headache settled to a dull throb, and by the time she got out of the shower, she was feeling marginally better. Kit forced her to eat some toast room service had brought up and drink some peppermint tea, which did wonders for her head and her energy level. The thought of marching into Slade's office was pretty invigorating, so maybe it wasn't the tea that woke her up and cleared the fog.

Kit had perfumed and aired out her taco T-shirt and paired it with a fitted black-and-white patterned skirt and some funky blue heels. Mae buttoned up a pink rayon shirt over her T-shirt so she would look professional going into Slade's office. When Kit finally pronounced her ready—after wasting far too much time on makeup, in Mae's opinion—they left the hotel and got an Uber to Slade's business building. Boston Commons was beautiful and green, and instead of the anxiety she'd thought she'd feel in an unfamiliar place, she felt excitement to explore.

Mae wanted to tour the historic city, hopefully with Slade as her tour guide. Hopefully. Did he think she'd ditched him last night? What else was he supposed to think?

Soon they pulled up to a tall glass-and-steel building in the financial district, close to the iconic Faneuil Hall. They thanked the driver and got out.

Kit tugged on Mae's hand. "No turning back now, baby."

Mae let her pull her through the doors and up to a reception area. They were informed that Steele Wholesale Lending took up floors twenty-one and twenty-two. The elevator ascended so quickly Mae was grateful for the toast and peppermint tea to help her belly. She was getting tired of being so stirred up all the time. Yet how could she calm down before she met Slade and tried to explain all the craziness she'd put him through? That was a tall order that she didn't know how to fill.

The receptionist who greeted them as they exited the elevator was friendly but reticent, a beautiful lady probably in her late fifties. "I'm sorry. Mr. Steele is very busy. Can I make you an appointment for ... four-thirty-five?" she asked.

"I'm Mae Delaney," she explained. "I've worked with Mr. Steele for the past two years as an account rep via video chat, and I'm here to meet him in person."

The receptionist's eyes registered recognition of her name. "I've heard of you, but he still doesn't have any openings."

No openings? No time for her. Slade always had time for her. Well, most of the time he was the one who initiated the calls because her schedule was almost always open, but it hurt that he couldn't fit her in. She felt insignificant and silly that she thought she could just waltz in here, give her name, and hope his important schedule would disappear.

"Please." Kit clasped her hands together. "You don't understand."

"Help me," the older lady said.

"Okay, it's like this," Kit said. "Slade flew to meet Mae—" She pointed to Mae, and Mae waved, wondering what Kit was going to spill in the next few seconds. "—in Sausalito, California, and it got all messed up and he thought she was someone else and he kind of fell for the wrong woman, even though it was really Mae. Then speed ahead with some flirting and confusion to pass the time ... he sent his jet for the real Mae so he could meet her last night, but her family was killed on Golden Gate Bridge and she's never flown in an airplane, so I gave her some Valium, but she took two instead of one and it made her so tired and crazy. Like she was drunk!" Kit paused for a breath.

People from offices were poking their heads out and Mae tried to shush Kit, but if it would get her in to Slade, she'd go through Public Humiliation 101.

"So, I finally decided I had to just take her to the hotel, but we lost her phone, so I couldn't even text or call Slade. She just needs him to see her and know she didn't ditch him again. Then we'll let him go back to his busy schedule. Please." Kit clasped her hands dramatically together and begged the woman with her big blue eyes.

Mae wanted to tell Kit those eyes only worked on the opposite sex, but she added her prayers to Kit's pleas and waited impatiently for the verdict.

The lady looked indecisive, but eventually she nodded. "Two minutes."

Kit squealed, and Mae jumped happily and miraculously didn't fall off her heels. "Thank you," Mae and Kit said together.

They hurried behind the woman, pumping up a wide, open staircase and toward an office at the end of the hall with double doors, obviously the biggest and most important office. Slade had been so down-to-earth and fun with her, and sometimes Mae forgot how successful and prominent he was.

The receptionist cast them one more worried glance before knocking on the door.

"Yes?" Slade called in response to the sharp rap.

"Tell him my name is Josie, please," Mae said quickly. Was that wrong? Poor Slade would be so confused. Oh man, she was nervous.

The receptionist looked even more baffled, but she nodded, cracked the door, peeked her head in, and said, "A *Josie* to see you, sir?"

"Josie?" He paused long enough for Mae's nerves to reach hyperdrive. Her palms started sweating and her heart raced. Seconds passed without any response at all.

The receptionist glanced back at Mae, compassion and the desire to do her job effectively warring in her brown eyes.

"Excuse me for interrupting you, sir," she said back through the door.

Mae's stomach dropped. She was right here, and she couldn't even see him. Tempted to dart through the door, Mae clenched her hands and teetered on her heels.

Clearing his throat, he said, "Send her in, please."

Relief rushed through her. The lady nodded to her, and Kit pushed her from the back. Mae stumbled in.

Slade stood behind his desk, staring at her as if she were an apparition. He looked amazing in a black suit with a striped black-and-white shirt and a pale blue tie. "Josie?"

She nodded, her tongue too thick in her mouth to talk. She was right here, he was right here, and she didn't know what to say. Would he hate her when he found out she'd lied? She was going to dissolve into a puddle of stress sweat if she didn't get the truth out soon.

"How did you find me?" A muscle worked in his jaw as if he was fighting to control himself. Was he upset, excited, concerned? She was all three at the moment.

"Well ..." She swallowed and muttered, "You're Slade Steele."

"So, you knew who I was that night?" He walked around his desk and toward her, stopping a foot away. His dark eyes were interested but wary. She'd envisioned him rushing to her and sweeping her off her feet.

"Yes," she muttered.

"Why didn't you say anything that night? Why haven't you contacted me before now? I wanted to see you again."

"Do you still want to?"

He pushed a hand through his hair, paused, and finally muttered, "I'm really confused. The woman I was supposed to meet the night I met you—the name I said after we kissed ..." He looked adorably embarrassed. Well, as adorable as the enigmatic, perfectly handsome Slade Steele could look. "She was supposed to fly in and meet me last night, and ..." He swallowed and glanced away. "She ditched me again."

His eyes swept over her carefully, longingly. "I haven't been able to find you, and I can't get the way I felt when I touched and kissed you out of my head, but there's something about Mae, and even with you right here, I still want to give her a chance. I'm sorry."

Mae's heart swelled. He'd felt a connection with Josie, but he still would give up a chance with her to meet Mae, who he thought had ditched him twice? He still wanted Mae, even with the beautiful Josie standing right in front of him? She almost cheered, but instead she muttered, "Funny story about that crazy Mae. She and I are actually ... close."

He blinked at her, obviously bewildered that Josie knew Mae and that she was bringing it up now. "Excuse me?"

Mae started unbuttoning her blouse, her hands trembling.

Slade held up his hands as if to protect himself from her undressing. "Stop!"

Mae laughed but sobered quickly as she was terrified what the next few seconds might bring. "I'm not stripping," she said.

His eyes widened, but he put his hands down as her T-shirt underneath showed. She pulled the other shirt off and dropped it; then she found her glasses in her purse and put them on, having to close her eyes so the double prescription didn't make her sick. Then she pulled her hair back from her face with her other hand.

She heard his sharp intake of breath. He knew. Was that a good intake of oxygen? A surprised one? In her dreams he'd rush across the space and hold her close, but real life rarely was like her dreams, except for the night she'd kissed him as Josie.

Releasing her hair and taking the glasses back off, she stowed them in her purse and awaited his reaction. Did he truly care for frumpy Mae, or had she just ruined all his illusions of the mysterious Josie and upset him because she'd hidden the truth from him?

His eyes flickered down to her T-shirt and back up to her face—desire, frustration, tenderness, and confusion all evident in his dark gaze.

"You up for tacos?" she managed to get out.

Slade crossed the distance between them so quickly that she gasped. He wrapped his arms around her lower back and leaned down. "Mae? You're Josie?"

She nodded, joy coursing through her veins. Of course Slade wouldn't be mad or treat her poorly. He was Slade Steele, the man of her every dream, and he really deserved an explanation of all this craziness.

She opened her mouth to give that explanation, but he cut it off by kissing her. The explosion of emotion his kiss created was stronger than it had been the first night she'd kissed him. He knew who she was, and he was choosing to forgive her quickly and show her with his lips exactly how interested he was in her. She felt so light that she could have floated away. Slade's mouth caressed hers and his arms held her close to his firm body. She loved him, and she wanted to tell him.

He slowed the kisses down and tenderly kissed her jawline until he reached her earlobe; then he whispered, "Why didn't you tell me?"

"I didn't know how."

He pulled back slightly, and his eyes reflected pain but also understanding. "I've been going through ..." He shook his head but thankfully didn't release her from his arms. "It's been rough, Mae. I was falling for the funny, adorable Mae, but I couldn't get the beautiful, mystical Josie out of my head. I still can't believe you're all ... one." He paused, giving her a chance to explain.

"I'm so sorry. I was a mess that night at the restaurant. When you didn't recognize me, I kind of flipped out and all my insecurities overwhelmed me. I couldn't imagine that the perfect Slade Steele would ever want Mae anyway, and then the waiter—Dirk? He encouraged me to give you a test to see if you'd fall for the beautiful lady or hold out for frumpy Mae."

"Please don't ever call yourself frumpy, Mae. Even with those glasses on you, were appealing to me."

"Thank you."

Someone rapped on the door.

"Yes?" Slade called, but he didn't release her from his arms.

The receptionist poked her head in. "Sir, your eleven-fifteen is here."

"I'm sorry, you're going to have to reschedule my appointments for ..." He gave Mae an irresistible and almost wicked grin. "At least the next week. John will be happy to step in."

The receptionist's eyes widened, but she nodded.

"Yes!" Kit hollered. "Yes, my girl did it!"

The door shut, and Slade tilted his head. "The blonde who was with you?"

"My best friend, Kit. I wouldn't be here without her."

"I can't wait to meet her, in a few minutes." He kissed her tenderly, but when he pulled back, his jaw tightened. "So Dirk manipulated you? The guy was hoping to have his own shot at dating you."

"It wouldn't have mattered. You're the only one I've ever wanted."

Slade grinned and kissed her soundly.

When they broke apart, Mae asked breathlessly, "Can you ever forgive me for not telling you the truth, and then the confusion last night? Kit gave me Valium to help me get over the bridge and on the plane. I took two instead of one, and it knocked me for a loop." She didn't want to get into all her issues about the bridge the first time she met the man of her future. Well, sort of the first time. Would he still want her if he knew about her past and her fears?

"Why are you afraid of the bridge and flying?"

Mae bit at her lip. Apparently, the issues would have to come up. "My parents and sisters were killed on the bridge. I've never flown before, and I haven't driven across the bridge since I was fourteen."

"I'm so sorry, Mae." His condolences were sincere, reflected by the pain he felt for her in his eyes.

"Thank you. I'm sorry my issues kept us apart."

"It's all right. We got here." He smiled. "You conquered your fears to be with me?"

She nodded. A rush of accomplishment overcame her, along with happiness that she was finally in his arms. "Yeah, I did." She took a steadying breath. "Will you please forgive me for all the craziness?"

Slade studied her. "On one condition."

"What's that?"

"You come with me to meet my little sister."

Meet his sister? She loved the commitment of that. She tilted her head. "On one condition."

"What's that?"

"You buy me a taco ... after you kiss me again."

Slade grinned. "I think I can handle those conditions."

His head bowed toward hers, and Mae clung to his neck as she proceeded to kiss him with all the desire she'd been storing up for him. His answering kiss told her he'd forgiven her for any craziness and he would be there when she had insecurities and fears. His touch brought a sense of excitement and home she hadn't felt since she was fifteen.

CHAPTER FOURTEEN

Slade had taken Mae and Kit to a late breakfast slash early lunch at a fabulous Mexican restaurant that specialized in street tacos. The entire story of Mae being Josie spilled out, with Kit throwing in all kinds of funny details, and they all laughed and enjoyed being together. It was the first time in Mae's life that a man hadn't gone gooey-eyed over Kit. She adored her beautiful blond friend, but she wasn't sharing Slade with anyone. He held her hand under the table every chance he got, and Mae knew she'd never been this happy.

After breakfast, Slade called his driver and they all walked out into the balmy summer morning. He squeezed Mae's hand. "Are you still okay to stay for a few days, or as long as I can keep you?"

She nodded, speechless. He wanted her to stay. The anticipation of spending more time with him felt like a tickling of warmth all over, like sliding into a hot bath with lavender-infused salts in it.

He glanced at Kit. "You're welcome to stay also."

"Oh, no." Kit held up her hands. "I am not the type to play the third wheel. I'll catch a flight back to San Fran as soon as there's an opening on standby."

"No," Slade said decisively. "I'll have a car take you to my airplane, and they'll fly you home."

"Whew!" Kit blew out a whistling breath. "You've got that sexy alpha male thing *down*."

"Kit!" Mae protested, but she completely agreed.

Slade chuckled and made another call. The cars arrived, and Mae hugged Kit goodbye. "Thank you for being the best friend ever," Mae said.

"I love you and I'm so happy right now." Kit squeezed her tight, then released her and shot Slade a look. "You might be a buff billionaire, but treat her right or I'll pay someone to hunt you down and cut your ears off."

"Whoa." Slade nodded obediently, then grinned. "I'll treat her right, because she's amazing … and I like my ears."

Kit winked, gave Mae one more hug, and slid into the car.

The driver of the other car opened the door. Mae slid into the middle seat, and Slade eased in next to her. Wrapping his arm around her, he said, "It's about a thirty-minute drive to my parents' house. You might as well kiss me to pass the time."

Mae laughed. "I guess we have to do something to stave off the boredom."

"For sure." He pulled her in tight and proceeded to kiss her. Mae forgot about the driver, the opportunity to check out the sites of Boston, and everything but his lips on hers.

When they pulled to a stop and the driver got out and came around to get the door, she was flushed and startled. "No way was that thirty minutes."

"Maybe traffic was light," he murmured.

"Or maybe I just like to kiss you."

He grinned and kissed her again.

Finally, Mae got embarrassed. "Your driver is going to think you're nuts."

"Naw. John likes me, right, John?"

"Yes, sir. And I don't blame you for kissing her for over forty minutes, either. Traffic was heavy."

Slade laughed as Mae's face flushed with heat. Slade slid out of the car and offered his hand, which she gleefully accepted; she loved the sparks she felt from simply touching his hand.

She thanked the driver and then turned with Slade to look at the gorgeous mansion in front of her. It was a classic Cape Cod style set right on a bluff above the ocean. "Guess your parents had money before you become a raving success?"

He smirked. "They do okay for themselves."

"Okay? This place is fabulous!" She shook her head, trying to hide how intimidated she was by his wealth and status. Could she truly fit in his world? "'It's one of my favorite planes,'" she said, quoting him from last night. "Stinking billionaire punk."

Slade's arm wrapped around her waist and he turned her toward him. "Take it back."

"Or what?" She hid her smile and arched an eyebrow.

"Or I'll kiss you until you do."

"You do that."

His mouth met hers, and she wondered if she'd ever get used to the explosion of joy, warmth, and desire that felt like fireworks in her soul. She thought maybe they should stop kissing where people might see them, but then she figured they were making up for lost time.

"Slade!" a girl's voice called from the porch.

They broke apart, but Slade kept his arm around Mae's waist as he escorted her through the gate and up the cobblestone path. "Lottie," he called. "I brought her."

"Josie or Mae?" She hurried down the porch steps to meet them, holding on to the railing for balance. She was a gorgeous teenage girl with long, dark hair, beautiful skin, and almond-shaped eyes that slanted slightly upward, characteristic of Down syndrome. She was dressed in a flowing pale blue sundress that set off her beautiful coloring.

"Both," Slade replied, grinning down at Mae.

Mae returned his smile.

His sister reached them, and after Slade gave her a hug, she turned and squeezed Mae tight around the waist. Mae was taken aback by the familiarity with someone she didn't know, but she instantly felt the sweetness of the girl's spirit and hugged her tightly back.

"Hi," Lottie said.

"It's nice to meet you, Lottie."

Lottie pulled back and demanded, "Now tell me 'bout you—both Josie and Mae?" Her brow squiggled.

Slade said, "This is a story for you, Lottie. Better than any of your girl movies."

"No!" Lottie's mouth pursed, and her eyes widened.

"It's the best story ever," Mae agreed.

"Well, then, tell it to me." Lottie put her hands on her hips.

"Of course." Mae paused to think of how to condense it. "I was ... in disguise the first time we met, and he didn't recognize me."

"Slade!" Lottie's tone was full of exasperation and reproof.

"She was more beautiful than any woman I'd ever met, and I'd only seen Mae with these huge glasses on that covered her eyes and part of her face," said Slade. "It wasn't completely my fault."

"But you kissed her." Lottie shook her head and pushed out a disgusted breath.

"I'm sorry, sis, but she was irresistible." He winked and squeezed Mae's waist. "In fact, I could kiss her right now." He leaned in close, and Mae's breath shortened.

"Story first," Lottie interrupted. She grinned and added, "Then I watch the kissing."

Slade gestured to her, and Mae continued, "When he didn't recognize me, I told him my name was Josie, and at first I was upset that he didn't recognize me as Mae, but he was so charming ... I think I might have kissed *him* that night."

"No," he interjected. "I definitely kissed you, and no kiss had ever been so powerful. Until the one in my office today." He winked. "And every one since then."

Heat filled Mae's body and she leaned into him. Maybe she didn't fit in his world, but Slade didn't seem to care, and all she cared about right now was being close to him.

"But when did you find out she was Mae?" Lottie asked.

"Just today," Slade told her, his eyes drinking in Mae.

"We kept missing each other," Mae tried to explain. "But now we've found each other."

"Yay! So Josie is Mae?" Lottie nodded as if she had it all figured out. "Which one you love?"

Fire burned through Mae. Love? Were they there? Of course she loved Slade, had for a long time, but could he possibly feel the same? She'd hardly dared imagine a world where her adoration of him was reciprocated.

"Josie is Mae," Slade reaffirmed. His dark gaze seared into her. "And I love them both."

"You ... love me?" Mae said faintly, her head whirling almost as bad as if she'd taken Valium again.

Slade nodded. "I know we just officially met, but despite the fact that I wasn't looking for you, I've fallen in love with you, Mae. The connection between us is unlike anything I've ever felt." He paused, then said, "You don't have to say it back, but I wanted you to know."

"Oh, I'll say it back." Mae slid close against him and framed his face with her hands. "I love you, Slade. I've loved you for two years, and now I'm going to do something about it."

He chuckled. "Oh yeah? What are you going to do?"

She grinned, anticipation and desire swirling in the heated air between them.

"Kiss her, you tater tot," Lottie called from the side, clapping her hands together and then waving them at her forehead. "It's time now!"

Mae had almost forgotten their audience, but she figured it would be like watching a movie for the darling girl. Hopefully Slade's parents wouldn't think it was indecent exposure or anything.

"I can do that." Slade swept Mae off her feet and proceeded to kiss her. As he deepened the kiss, every part of her body was flooded with delightful warmth. Mae wondered if this kiss might classify as over the top for a teenage girl to watch, but she was too wrapped up in it to come back down to earth.

Slade loved her. Nothing else mattered at the moment.

CHAPTER FIFTEEN

Mae stood in Lottie's sun-filled bedroom with her stomach twisting into knots. She'd wrongly assumed that once she'd connected with Slade, the anxiousness would disappear. With Slade by her side, she felt happy and light as if nothing could go wrong, but right now he was downstairs waiting for her with his brothers; all three of them had flown in for the weekend specifically to meet her and to attend a dinner party where Mae would meet other close friends and family.

Slade's mom and dad had been friendly, warm, and open with her. Though they were both dressed up all the time and obviously were in a different socioeconomic class than she'd ever associated with, they treated her as if she were the future daughter-in-law they'd always wanted. Future daughter-in-law. She gulped and pressed a hand to her stomach. She and Slade had only been together for the past few days: they'd played tourist and guide in the beautiful city and surrounding areas, worked together at his office, and simply enjoyed each other's company. They weren't even close to engaged, and she needed to stop daydreaming and finish getting ready.

Lottie burst into the room, wearing a lacy peach-colored sheath dress with her dark hair in long curls. "You look *so-o* beautiful!"

"So do you."

Lottie wrinkled her nose. "I always look beautiful."

Mae smiled. She loved Lottie's confidence and infectious happiness. She had been finishing getting ready in the bathroom earlier when Lottie banged on the door to tell her she'd be right back after she hugged her "boys," as she called her brothers. Now she was back, and that was probably Mae's cue to head downstairs.

Mae glanced at the full-length white-trimmed mirror. She was wearing one of the dresses Kit had sent with her. It was red and white polka-dotted, sleeveless, fitted at the waist, and a couple inches above the knee. She felt pretty, but it was a brave dress for her with the bright color and shorter hemline. Was it wrong that she preferred wearing dark colors and being in the shadows? She wouldn't be able to hide tonight, and if it weren't for Slade, she didn't know that she'd even attempt going down those stairs.

"Let's go." Lottie tugged at her hand.

Mae's high-heeled feet stayed planted on the wood floor.

"What's wrong?" Lottie faced her, her lovely brow wrinkled.

"I don't know if I can do this," Mae admitted.

"Do what?"

"Meet your brothers, meet all these people tonight. I'm not brave and confident like you and Slade." Mae glanced out the huge windows at the ocean down below, embarrassed that she'd admitted so much to her new friend.

"Mae, you silly." Lottie laughed, and Mae focused on her. "First, my boys are not to be scared of. They love you ... just like Slade loves you."

Mae bit at her lip, thinking first Lottie couldn't understand how powerful, successful, and intimidating her family was, and second that they'd better not love her just like Slade did, or Slade would probably get in a fight tonight. Of course the sweet girl didn't mean it like that. Slade did love her. The remembrance brought peace and helped settle her stomach.

"But also, Mae ..." Lottie shook her long curls. "You don't really know. I'm not brave or feel beautiful always. At school? Sometimes, kids make fun."

Mae's stomach twisted again. Who could be callous or mean enough to make fun of Lottie?

"My mama taught me something. She said ..." Lottie screwed up her mouth as if remembering. "Everybody's trying to find their spot." Lottie nodded. "Close enough. And when someone makes fun, it's 'cause they don't feel good about themself. Right?"

Mae hadn't had a mom to help her navigate high school, but Kit's mom would've probably said something similar. Mae had made it through high school hiding in Kit's shadow, and she'd been perfectly content with it.

"But the most important things? Like yourself and like everybody else. If you like yourself, it no matter what they say, and if you like everybody else, they stop being mean."

Mae blinked at her. Tears pricked the corners of her eyes. She reached out and hugged Lottie tight.

Lottie squeezed her back. "That help?"

"Yes, sweet girl. You are amazing." Like yourself and like everybody else. It was her Christian philosophy to love everyone, but sometimes you could love others without really liking them, and it was really hard to be confident and comfortable with who she was. Like yourself. It could be that simple. If she was confident in herself and in Slade's love for her, it really didn't matter how tonight went. Slade wouldn't ditch her if she tripped on her heels or said something dumb to one of his famous brothers or friends. Closing her eyes, she said a brief prayer of gratitude for Slade and Lottie, followed by a prayer that she could like herself as well as everyone else.

"All right." Lottie pulled from the hug, clasped Mae's hand, and said, "Let's go. Slade is a mess down there!"

This time Mae let Lottie tug her out of the bedroom and into the wide hallway. "Why is Slade a mess?" Slade was always confident and perfect. Always.

"You'll see."

They were at the top of the wide staircase now, and voices floated up from down below, so Mae didn't have a chance to grill Lottie about why Slade would be a mess. They descended the stairs, slowly. Lottie didn't move fast on stairs, and Mae was grateful with the black heels she wore threatening to take her down.

A few steps from the bottom, Mae heard Slade's voice. "Mae."

The way he said her name, all breathy and longing, made her heart thump faster and her stomach swirl with delicious heat. She glanced up to smile at him, tripped, and went flying.

"Mae!" Lottie yelled, and luckily their hands sprung apart so Mae didn't pull her down.

She hit the floor, catching herself with her hands and groaned. Embarrassment rushed in quickly as her dress had flung all the wrong directions, but only her palms stung from the impact.

"Mae." Slade rushed to her side and squatted down close. "Are you okay? Is anything hurt?"

"Just my pride and dignity, and they are pros at taking a thumping."

She heard laughter and focused on Slade's handsome face. He grinned at her. "Can I pick you up, or will that injure your pride and dignity further?"

"Hmm, you're cute enough I will allow you to sweep me into your arms."

Slade chuckled and obeyed. He wrapped his arms around her waist and plucked her off the ground. Holding her close, he tilted her chin so she focused on him and not the rest of the room, who'd all unfortunately witnessed her clumsiness.

"You look so beautiful," he murmured, his eyes tracing over her face.

"Really? Sprawled on the floor with my dress over my head, I looked beautiful?"

Some deep chuckles came from far too close by, and Mae wanted to look to see if there was shock or disgust on Slade's brothers' faces. Were they laughing at her, or with her?

"It was a great look on you." He winked and turned her to face his family.

His parents, Lottie, and all three of his brothers smiled kindly at her, as if they wanted to see the best in her. She could feel the love they had for Slade through those kind looks.

"You still like you, right, Mae?" Lottie asked.

"Some days it's rough, my sweet friend," Mae said.

"Nope. Every day you like you." She gestured around. "These are my boys!" She clapped her hands together and then waved them at her forehead excitedly.

Slade still had his arm around her waist, but his mom, Sarah, came forward and gave Mae a hug. "You look beautiful, dear. I'm so thrilled to have you here with us."

"Thank you." Mae was teary-eyed again. How could Slade's mom be so kind and so perfect at the same time? Mae might be the dowdy girl next to her, but Sarah only radiated love and acceptance.

Slade's dad came forward and shook her hand. He looked a lot like his boys, well-built and handsome, but his dark hair was interspersed with lighter gray. His dark eyes twinkled. "Sarah and

Lottie have been waiting for another female in the family for a long time."

"Vince," Sarah reprimanded, but Mae didn't mind the insinuation. Not at all.

Slade's hand tightened around her waist as his three brothers stepped toward them. They were all dressed in button-down shirts and slacks. With their dark hair and eyes, smooth, tanned skin, and short facial hair, they closely resembled Slade.

"Okay. I've got these guys down. I've been studying," Mae said, hoping for some of the confidence Lottie had infused in her upstairs. "Preston, the football hero."

Preston chuckled and shook her hand. "Yes, ma'am."

"Don't mind his fake Southern drawl," Slade said. "He's been in Georgia too long and thinks it'll get him dates."

Preston shrugged. "I have to beat the groupies off with a stick."

"I'm sure you do." Mae laughed, then nodded to the next brother. "Gunner, the military hero."

He shook her hand, his smile a little more solemn than his obviously mischievous brothers. Mae wondered what he'd seen in his time with the SEALs. "Pleasure to meet you, Mae."

"You too." She turned to the last one. "Jex, the crazy man."

Everyone but Jex exploded in laughter. "Aw, come on," Jex complained. "Preston and Gunner are 'heroes.' The way you look at Slade is like he's the most perfect man on the planet, and I'm crazy?"

Mae lifted her hands innocently. "Sorry, but I have been watching your YouTube videos. Crazy is a mild way to describe you."

They all laughed again. Slade nodded to his brothers, and they each took a large step back and started unbuttoning their shirts.

"Boys!" Sarah cried out.

Lottie grabbed her mother's hand. "It's okay, Mama. Just watch." She grinned broadly at Mae. "You can watch too. It's PG-rated."

"Not my chest," Jex said. "It's at least PG-13."

"Oh, Jex," Lottie giggled.

They pulled their shirts off and tossed them on a nearby couch. Mae felt Slade's arm tense around her waist as she read each t-shirt in order of how they were standing.

Preston's said, "Mae, let's taco 'bout marrying Slade." Gunner's said, "I'm nacho type, but Slade is." Jex's read, "In queso you missed it, Slade wants to marry you."

"Oh, boys," Sarah said with a soft sigh.

"Yes!" Lottie cheered.

Mae's heart was thumping so hard she couldn't catch a breath. It appeared that Slade's brothers not only accepted her but were willing to ask her to marry him.

Slade turned her toward him and gave her an irresistible, but hesitant grin. He looked as nervous as Mae felt. Taking a step back, he slowly unbuttoned his shirt. His smoldering look was so appealing that she couldn't help but reach out to him.

She forgot they weren't alone until his mom said, "Slade. You don't have to look all ... sexy."

"I don't mind," Mae piped up.

"Of course you don't," Jex said.

Her cheeks tinged with color as Slade laughed easily. Mae's stomach swooped when he pulled the button-down shirt off. He was wearing a fitted gray shirt that read in bold white letters, "I love you, Mae. Marry me?"

Slade dropped to one knee and pulled a ring out of his pocket. Mae forced herself to look at the sparkling round diamond, but her gaze was drawn quickly back to Slade's face. His dark eyes were filled with love for her and begged her to say yes.

"Please say you'll marry me, Mae," he said.

Mae dropped onto her knees in front of him and cupped his face. "Of course I will. Yes!"

"Kiss her, you tater tot!" Lottie yelled.

Mae ignored the laughter as she kissed him, about toppling them both onto the floor. Slade steadied them and stood, pulling her up with him. He gently slid the ring on her finger and then pulled her in close, taking possession of her mouth just as surely as he had her heart.

When they pulled back, she noticed Gunner was shifting uncomfortably, but the rest of the group was laughing at them. Lottie rushed to a nearby cupboard and pulled out more T-shirts. She handed them out. Sarah's said, "Proud Steele Mama."

Vince's said, "Tough as Steele Daddy." Lottie's said, "I'm the Steele Princess." Lottie handed a pink T-shirt to Mae.

"Thank you." Mae unfolded it, her gorgeous diamond glinting in the light. Her T-shirt said, "Tough enough to get a Steele to his knees." Mae laughed. "I love it. Thank you."

Her eyes glistened as she glanced around the room at the brothers all wearing their T-shirts for her and the rest of the group holding T-shirts. It was thoughtful and endearing and put her at ease. Well, as at ease as she could be as a newly engaged woman to the enigmatic, charming, and handsome man smiling down at her.

"Can we wear them for the party?" Lottie asked her mom.

Everyone turned to Sarah. Mae had noticed that Sarah was very loving and down-to-earth, but she also was always dressed impeccably and kept her house spotless. She wouldn't want her family wearing goofy T-shirts, some of which would make no sense to an outsider, for a fancy dinner party.

"It's all right," Mae started. "We can wear them another day."

"Of course we're wearing them for the party," Sarah said, smiling kindly at Mae. "Let's go get changed; the guests will be here soon."

Slade directed Mae out one of the rear patio doors. There was a large outdoor tent set up outside with a buffet all ready. Mae could see heating elements under some of the food and other food containers on ice. "Wow. Your mom is ready for a party."

He tugged her close. "I'm only ready for you." His voice dropped huskily. "I love you, Mae. Thank you for agreeing to marry me."

Mae laughed and cupped his jaw with one hand, her T-shirt balled in her other fist. "I love you, Slade. Thank you for asking."

The kiss they shared pushed everything else from her mind.

When they heard laughter and throats clearing, they broke apart. Mae looked sheepishly around at a crowd of people she didn't know. "Wow, the guests must've come early," she murmured.

"Everybody's actually late," Jex said from behind them.

Mae laughed. "You try kissing him and you'd lose track of time too."

Jex pulled a face. "I'll take your word for it." He winked and strode off to greet some people.

"Slade," several of the group called out.

He waved but stayed close to Mae.

Mae held up her shirt. "Shall I go change?"

Slade took it from her and tugged it over her head. Mae shrugged into the sleeves and laughed as the baggier T-shirt covered the top of her dress, but with a pink T-shirt and a red polka-dot dress, she looked ridiculous. She was meeting all of Slade's close friends and family. Kit would be appalled.

"I can't wear it like this," she protested.

Slade kissed her softly and said, "You look perfect. I love you." Then he took her hand and turned to start greeting people.

Mae caught Sarah's eye and pointed to her outfit. Sarah smiled and gave her a thumbs-up, looking classy and yet approachable in her t-shirt paired with a fitted blue skirt. Mae's last fear disappeared. Slade's family not only accepted her; they embraced her, quirky T-shirts and all.

Slade squeezed her waist and grinned proudly at her as he introduced her to someone—she thought she heard "Senator" somewhere in the title. She realized she should be intimidated, but the distinguished-looking man had a large smile for her, and she shook his hand with her own smile in place. Slade was by her side. She could handle anything with his arm around her.

I hope you loved Mae and Slade's story. I had so much fun writing it. My husband told me I giggled as I wrote. I patterned sweet Lottie after my darling niece, Lexi Lynn, who brings so much light and love to our family.

Kit's story is also delightful and nonstop fun. *Her Prince Charming Boss* will be out soon, followed by Slade's brother Preston's story in the next Georgia Patriots Romance.

Thank you so much for reading and all of the unreal support. I love my fans!

Hugs,

Cami

ABOUT THE AUTHOR

Cami is a part-time author, part-time exercise consultant, part-time housekeeper, full-time wife, and overtime mother of four adorable boys. Sleep and relaxation are fond memories. She's never been happier.

Join Cami's VIP list to find out about special deals, giveaways and new releases and receive a free copy of *Rescued by Love: Park City Firefighter Romance* by clicking here.

Read on for short excerpts of Cami's latest Texas Titans Romance and the start of the Quinn Family Romance, *The Devoted Groom: Quinn Family Romance* and a short excerpt of another Billionaire Boss and Quinn Family Romance*: Her Too-Perfect Boss.*

Happy reading!

cami@camichecketts.com
www.camichecketts.com

EXCERPT - THE DEVOTED GROOM

Bree reached the ten-foot wooden door and squared her shoulders. Raising a hand to knock, she jumped when the door swung open. "Balls of pelican poop!" She put a hand to her chest. "Sorry, you scared me!"

Ryder Quinn stood on the threshold, holding a towheaded little boy in one arm and smiling at her as if she were a circus performer.

Bree took a step back. He was bigger than she'd envisioned. At least six four, and every line of his body was defined. She prayed he was as kind as everyone claimed, otherwise the sheer strength of him was a huge warning flag to her.

She took a deep breath and forced a smile, fluffing her hair before sticking her hand out. "Bree Stevens." That sounded professional, right? Not like she was barely out of college and not sure how to present herself?

Ryder's eyes swept over her. She'd heard he was sought after by many women but he never gave anyone a second look. The speculation was he still mourned his wife. It was hard to blame the women for trying though. His blue eyes were framed with long, brown lashes. His face was sculpted and shadowed by a trimmed beard a few shades darker than his short sandy-blond hair. His lips were almost as incredible as his eyes, a slightly-bowed upper lip with a fuller lower lip. She could imagine the women fought for the sheer hope of tasting those incredible lips.

Those lips she was staring at turned up, and he shifted the little boy higher as he offered his hand to Bree. "Welcome." It was just one word, two syllables. How could he draw it out and make it all warm and appetizing? As if he were welcoming her to be part of his life, to privileges and blessings she'd never dreamed of.

Snap out of it. She tried for a professional smile and put her hand in his. *Wowie, wow, wow!* His warm and slightly rough palm felt so manly and perfect against hers she wanted to just hold on. His gaze sharpened on her as if he felt the same connection that was racing through her. For some insane reason she felt like this man would protect her rather than objectify her. She had to remind herself that she didn't know him and she needed to tread carefully.

"Ryder Quinn," he murmured.

Bree pulled her hand back and chuckled uneasily. "I know who *you* are." She put her usual sass in the syllables. She'd acquired a lot of sass and some decent fighting skills to keep her mostly safe in foster care, rough schools, and college.

He smiled deeper, and she tilted to the side, needing something to lean on. Unfortunately, there was nothing, and her heels had her tilting even further. She would've fallen into the flower bed if Ryder hadn't grabbed her with his free hand and steadied her.

"You okay?" He arched an eyebrow, clearly thinking she was a bit unstable.

Be professional. Be professional. Bree smoothed down her silky floral shirt and blue pencil skirt. "Yes, thank you." She focused on the adorable boy in Ryder's arms. "And who is this handsome little man?"

Find *The Devoted Groom* here.

HER TOO-PERFECT BOSS

Navy took a break from freestyle and changed to breaststroke. She loved the warm water gliding past her body and decided she would swim all the way around the small island. If she got lucky, she'd see Holden sailing in once she made it around to the south.

Water rhythmically splashed behind her and Navy turned to look. A man was swimming toward her with quick, powerful strokes. Her first reaction was panic, thinking Ryan was chasing her. She didn't think the buff trainer would try to attack her, but she had never let herself be alone with him, just in case. Out here at the rear of the island, she could hardly even see the house. There would be no help coming if it was Ryan or another man who might hurt her.

Looking closer, she realized the man's coloring was much darker than Ryan's. She'd assumed it was only the *Muscle Up* crew on the island this week but maybe there was a caretaker? She squinted, wondering if it might be Holden, but she couldn't be sure. Whoever it was they must be some swimmer to be moving that fast.

She wasn't willing to risk being alone with an unknown man so she fell back into swimming and pushed herself around the back of the island, hoping she could make it to the bay where Holden's yacht would pull in soon and everyone would be busy unloading supplies. Her brother, Griff, a former Navy SEAL had taught her how to protect herself, but he'd been adamant that the best protection was to never be in a situation where a man could take advantage of her. She was tough, but she was small, and men were naturally stronger.

"Navy!"

She surfaced at sound of the familiar voice calling her name. The man had gained on her quickly and now was treading water a short distance away and grinning at her. The air rushed out of her body and Navy was grateful for the saltiness of the water making it easier to stay afloat. Holden Jennings was here and apparently chasing her around the island in the water. It might not mean anything to him, but it made her heart beat faster. He probably wanted to have a business meeting. In the gorgeous Caribbean ocean. In swimsuits. This water was really warm. She was sweating and splashed some water on her cheeks.

"Hey," she called back.

Holden did the breaststroke toward her, giving her the advantage of staring at his lovely shoulders and arms as he swam and his even lovelier face and smile as he approached. "Lovely" was a silly word to describe such a tough and perfectly handsome man, but she liked to use it. She could convince herself that "lovely" was mocking her perfect boss. He was *too* perfect. That was his fault. His manners were impeccable; he was wealthy, accomplished, hard-working, kind, funny. ... Too perfect. She definitely didn't want a man who was too perfect. How boring would that be? Boring or not, she couldn't resist staring and sighing softly as he got closer.

"How are you?" he asked as he finally reached her. She suddenly felt stupid. She'd made him swim the entire distance toward her as she treaded water and stared unabashedly at him.

"Fabulous. You?" Navy slowly milled her legs and arms in the water.

"Better now," he said, his grin growing. "Isn't she beautiful?"

"The island?"

But he wasn't looking at the island. He was staring straight at her. Holden gave a short laugh and splashed some water at her. "Yes, the island."

Navy dragged her arm through the water and gave him a mouthful. "Not as beautiful as that," Navy yelled, surprising herself with her impetuous response. She'd longed to be impetuous with this man and given the slightest opportunity, impetuous came very naturally.

Holden's eyes widened and then narrowed mischievously. Navy had seen that look on one of her brother's faces far too often. She dodged away, but Holden caught hold of her arm and dragged her under the water.

Navy came up spluttering. Holden chuckled. "Teach you to throw water at me."

"Oh, I'll teach you."

———

Keep reading here.

ALSO BY CAMI CHECKETTS

Quinn Family Romance

The Devoted Groom

The Conflicted Warrior

The Gentle Patriot

The Tough Warrior

Her Too-Perfect Boss

Her Forbidden Bodyguard

Hawk Brothers Romance

The Determined Groom

The Stealth Warrior

Her Billionaire Boss Fake Fiance

Risking it All

Navy Seal Romance

The Protective Warrior

The Captivating Warrior

The Stealth Warrior

Texas Titan Romance

The Fearless Groom

The Trustworthy Groom

The Beastly Groom

The Irresistible Groom

The Determined Groom

The Devoted Groom

Billionaire Beach Romance

Caribbean Rescue

Cozumel Escape

Cancun Getaway

Trusting the Billionaire

How to Kiss a Billionaire

Onboard for Love

Shadows in the Curtain

Billionaire Bride Pact Romance

The Resilient One

The Feisty One

The Independent One

The Protective One

The Faithful One

The Daring One

Park City Firefighter Romance

Rescued by Love

Reluctant Rescue

Stone Cold Sparks

Snowed-In for Christmas

Echo Ridge Romance

Christmas Makeover

Last of the Gentlemen

My Best Man's Wedding

Change of Plans

Counterfeit Date

Snow Valley

Full Court Devotion: Christmas in Snow Valley

A Touch of Love: Summer in Snow Valley

Running from the Cowboy: Spring in Snow Valley

Light in Your Eyes: Winter in Snow Valley

Romancing the Singer: Return to Snow Valley

Fighting for Love: Return to Snow Valley

Other Books by Cami

The Loyal Patriot: Georgia Patriots Romance

Seeking Mr. Debonair: Jane Austen Pact

Seeking Mr. Dependable: Jane Austen Pact

Saving Sycamore Bay

How to Design Love

Oh, Come On, Be Faithful

Protect This

Blog This

Redeem This

The Broken Path

Dead Running

Dying to Run

Fourth of July

Love & Loss

Love & Lies

Cami's Collections

Cami's Military Collection

Billionaire Beach Romance Collection

Billionaire Bride Pact Collection

Billionaire Romance Sampler

Echo Ridge Romance Collection

Texas Titans Romance Collection

Snow Valley Collection

Christmas Romance Collection

Made in the USA
Monee, IL
17 July 2023

39099312R00089